Arizona Tales

Volume One

Palace Poker
Mayer Daze
Into the Dark

THANKS FOR
BEING A GREAT GUY
LOVE

By Zeke Crandall *Zeke*

3-7-0-6

Preface

This preface is more like a disclaimer. Please, let it be known right now that I do not consider myself a writer. I am a storyteller, that simple. I hope to inspire all of my readers to write their stories, because without those stories a part of our past will be forgotten. My focus is to bring back to life some of Arizona's history. Many of these sites have been bypassed over time. I will be using those places as settings in my stories. The stories have been relayed to me second or third hand, so I must then call them historical fiction because I was not there and cannot verify for sure that they happened exactly as I was told.

I would like to take a moment to thank all of the folks that have come and gone, that were inspirational in my life. I would like to thank my wife, Rose and our five children, my mother, Beth, and my father, George. My father had a marvelous memory, a gift he passed on to me. I would like to thank my mother for being so patient with me when I was a child, and I was most definitely a handful. I also thank my little sister Cathy and my little brother George.

I would like to thank Kenny Harris. Kenny was my adopted Arizona grandfather and taught me how to fish, hunt and shoot as a small child. He was a real outdoorsman and took me everywhere with him. He was also a musician - a fiddle player. He and his friend Rudy, a banjo player, would take me with them to music gigs across the state. Through them I was able to meet a lot of old west characters and to travel all over the state of Arizona.

I think probably the most influential person in my life has been Tom McCarthy, my father-in-law. He is without a doubt the most creative and talented individual that I've ever met. We have had our differences over the years but there has never been any doubt about his focus. He is a real family man and he has always been there for our family. I would like to thank him for all of the art in this book - the cover and the introductory drawings before each story.

I would also like to thank Bill McCarthy for helping me edit my stories and also for being a great positive influence in my life. I would like to thank another Tom McCarthy, who happens to have the same name, but is no relation to my father- in-law. He is a retired Chicago police homicide detective and his expertise was invaluable as he helped edit "Mayer Daze". He has been a wealth of knowledge and it is a privilege to call him a friend.

I want to thank Rose Vyles for formatting these stories. A man must know his limitations and I simply am not an editor. (Remember, as I said earlier, I am a storyteller- not a writer.) I also would like to thank Debbie Wenig for her help, as well, in formatting "Palace Poker".

I would like to thank Keith Parks, my first boss at Cummins Diesel. Keith was a great influence on me by sharing his perfectionist attitude. He has had tremendous work habits throughout his life and, in my youth, helped me to become successful in all work endeavors. He has also been a good friend over the years.

I would like thank Melissa Ruffner and the staff at Sharlot Hall Museum, Archives Division, in Prescott, Arizona for their help with my research; Ron Abrahams and the Team Graphics staff in Glendale, Arizona, for helping me with the first print of this book; Bob and Beverly Drake, the owners of the Prescott Museum and Trading Company in Prescott, for helping me with my old time photos.

I believe this statement from my wife Rose to my first manager and good friend at Insight, Dan Betcher, says it all. "With Zeke, there will be good and there will be bad, but the good will out weigh the bad and there will never be a dull moment in between!" This pretty much sums up my life and writing style.

I have taken the time to dedicate each story to a person that was a big influence in my life. My wife has told me time and time again that I am her grownup ADD child. I am not sure that I have the ability to write a full novel, however, I do have many stories, that I will be sharing with my readers in future volumes of Arizona Tales. These are the first three. I hope you enjoy reading them as much as I enjoyed writing them. I hope they provide a little stress relief in your life. We all have too much stress in our lives today.

Thank You
Zeke Crandall

PALACE POKER

Palace Poker

By

Zeke Crandall
October 10, 2001

In Memory of
Kenny Harris

Chapter One
The Trip

It was Monday, November 3, 1957, and I was eleven years old. My Arizona Grandfather, Kenny Harris, was in the kitchen having a cup of tea while my mother prepared dinner. My sister Cathy and I had just arrived home from school. We walked home because our school, JB Sutton, was only about a half mile northeast on Roosevelt at 31st Avenue. We lived just north of Van Buren Street, on Taylor Street in Phoenix.

Kenny and Mary Harris, his wife, lived right across the street. They had adopted our family because they had no immediate family living in Arizona. They came from Cincinnati, Ohio and moved into the house across the street three years earlier. Our mother, Beth, told me to go in and clean up the bedroom as my little brother George had really messed it up. When I finished, I was to come back out to the kitchen to discuss the coming weekend.

Kenny was planning on going to Prescott that coming Saturday. My mother had agreed to let me join him and his banjo-playing buddy Rudy McDonald for the weekend. I went right in the room and picked up the mess without saying a word. After I finished, I proceeded back to the kitchen and sat down at the kitchen table with Kenny while my mother finished preparing our dinner. As I recall, she had a roast of beef cooking in the oven. She was also cooking mashed potatoes and green beans. We were all excited about dinner. My mother had invited Kenny and Mary to join us. We were just waiting for my father, George, to come home from work.

Kenny told me that he and Rudy would be heading to Prescott and that they had a gig on the coming Friday and Saturday night. He said that they had worked it out so that the three of us could spend the night at the St. Michael's Hotel right down the street from the Palace Saloon, which was on Whiskey Row. The St. Michael's sat on the southeast corner of Gurley and Montezuma.

The Palace Saloon was just about three establishments south of the St Michael's, on the west side of Montezuma Street. The city capital was actually the Arizona state capital in the late 1800's for several years before the capital was moved back to Phoenix. He said that the city had a big antique auction planned for the weekend and the owner of the Palace was expecting large crowds each night at the bar.

The Palace Saloon was one of the original bars on Whiskey Row in Prescott Arizona, along with Matt's Saloon, the Bird Cage Saloon and the Montezuma Bar. Kenny said that he thought I would really enjoy this historic small town. He said that the weather would be about twenty degrees cooler than Phoenix and that I needed to bundle up with winter clothes.

Kenny knew I would really enjoy the history of the Palace Bar. We had moved to Arizona from London, in Ontario, Canada. I was really into the western movies and just living in Arizona was a thrill. I could not wait to go to Prescott. I had read about the town and I knew it was rich in history. Kenny told me his friend, the bartender at the Palace, was an expert on the history of Prescott.

Kenny said that the town's people passed a law that limited the location of the saloon and bar establishments to one street, Montezuma, so as to not create any outbursts in the town neighborhoods. They also wanted all of the bars located on one street to keep the drunks and gamblers in one area, as they were considered bar patrons, and to cut policing expenses. I was really excited and asked Kenny when we were leaving. He told me I needed to be ready to go by 4:00 p.m. on the coming Friday. He told me to pack for two days and that we would be heading home right after breakfast on Sunday morning.

That Friday came very quickly. I rushed home from school dragging my poor little sister by the hand. I had already packed my bag for the weekend. My mother went through the bag with me, and sure enough, I had not packed enough socks or underwear. She told me that it might snow or rain and that I needed to prepare for possible bad weather. Just as we finished I heard a car honk. I looked out the window and there was Rudy in the passenger side front seat and Kenny in the driver's seat of Kenny's 1955 light blue AMC Rambler. My mom and sister kissed me goodbye. My mother told me to not get into any trouble and stay close to Kenny and Rudy.

Kenny told me that there was no room in the trunk for my bags because the musical instruments, microphones and amps were taking up the full area of the trunk. Rudy opened the door and pulled back the front seat so that I could sit in the back. I put the bag in the back seat and there still was room for me to sit along with the banjo that was too big to fit in the trunk.

By the time we left Phoenix it was 4:30 p.m. Kenny said we needed to hurry because they had to set up their amps and mics and be ready at 8:00 that evening. Prescott is 90 miles northeast of Phoenix. We arrived at 7:00 and I helped them unload the instruments and carry them into the saloon. Interestingly enough, it had the old type swinging bar doors just like in the old west.

As Kenny and Rudy were setting up their instruments I wandered around the saloon. The bartender saw me walking around and he explained the pictures on the walls. There were pictures of Wyatt Earp, Doc Holliday, and Little Egypt, a belly dancer around the turn of the century who had never been to Egypt.

We stopped at a picture of Virgil Earp. The bartender said that Virgil ran a saw mill there in Prescott just a year before he headed to Tombstone. There was also a picture of Big Nosed Kate, who was Doc Holliday's female traveling partner. Boy, it was obvious how she got her name. She had a big nose and a big body to match. She was not going to win any beauty contest to say the least.

After I looked around, I sat at the bar. Kenny came over and introduced me to the bartender. As it turned out, Kenny and Rudy were good friends of the bartender whose name was

Bill Campbell. Kenny told me that Bill was the person that we had talked about. He was the man with an incredible knowledge of Prescott. Bill was a man about 6'1" tall and weighed probably somewhere around 180 lbs. He was in his late 70s and had white hair with a full white beard.

Bill was a very friendly person with tremendous knowledge of the history of Prescott and of Arizona. Kenny told me not to bother him right then because it was about to get busy. He said that Bill had agreed to spend quite a bit of time filling me in on some old Prescott stories. He told me that Saturday morning would be best because it was slow in the morning and early afternoon.

By 9:00 p.m. the place was packed. The guys were playing their country music and folks were dancing in the back area. The dance area was very large, probably thirty by forty feet. As you walked into the saloon, the bar was to your left and was made of mahogany and extended about fifty feet. There were gambling tables along the right wall and several other small tables just to the left of the gambling tables.

I noticed that the safe was built into the wall. Just past the bar was the dance floor with tables on the left and on the right of the dance floor. I could not believe it, but the place was rocking by 9:30. I stayed until about 10:30 which was the first music break. We headed over to the hotel to check in. The guys hurried back to the saloon and I unloaded our bags and took them to our room. After I unpacked everything, I headed back to the saloon.

We had a great time. I could not get over the pure beauty of the bar. It had huge mirrors and mahogany pillars about every ten feet. There were several old guns hanging all along the back area. The seats were also made of mahogany. Bill said this was the original bar.

In 1900 there had been a big fire. Bill said all of the mirrors and the mahogany behind the bar had been removed from the bar just before the fire burned down the entire city block. The owners had time to take the whole bar and all of the wood and mirrors down. They took them outside to a safe place along with all of the tables and chairs as a precaution in case the fire spread. As it turned out the fire gutted the whole building. They were able to rebuild using all of the original tables, chairs, mirrors, the mahogany pillars and the bar itself. As I sat at the bar, I noticed a lot of round areas that were discolored under the bar. Bill told me that they were bullet holes that had been filled and patched as well as possible.

He said that Prescott had a little more class than Tombstone. He said that they filled the bullet holes in Prescott and finished staining them. He said that in Tombstone that the bars just let the holes stay. He said they thought that the holes gave the bars character.

He told me that he was too busy to go into detail, but asked me to come in tomorrow. He had a story that was told to him by his father when he was just a child and he just knew it would excite me. He really struck deep when he said that the story involved some of the folks whose pictures were on the walls around the saloon.

I was just too tired to stay awake any longer. It had been a long day for me and I was dead tired. I headed for our room at eleven. I was asleep when my head hit the pillow. It was definitely cooler in Prescott and I was very happy that I had brought my pajamas. I slept on a rollaway bed and there were two other single beds in the room for the guys.

Chapter Two
Saturday Morning

I woke up at 8:00 a.m. the next morning, which was Saturday. Rudy and Kenny were still sleeping. I got up, cleaned up, brushed my teeth, combed my hair and got dressed. I headed down the stairway to the hotel restaurant to eat breakfast. I had ten dollars that I had saved from my paper route tips and I felt like a rich man. I finished breakfast and went out for a little walk. I walked by the Palace and headed south on Montezuma. It was closed but I just could not help myself. I had to go up and peek inside at the pictures on the wall again.

I was really excited about listening to Bill tell me an old west story. I wandered into the Bird Cage Saloon. It was only about a third of the size of the Palace. The owner told me that the original owner of the Bird Cage Saloon was from Tombstone and he named the bar after the one he owned in Tombstone. On the right side wall I noticed there were five four foot by four foot glass cases with stuffed birds from all over the west. Over the bar was a collection of decorator whiskey bottle decanters, depicting famous west characters.

It was a little different and definitely a working class saloon. After I walked through the bar I headed back to our room at the hotel. The guys were just getting up. It was about 10 a.m. Kenny asked me where I had been. Rudy, started to laugh, and said, "Kenny, where do you think he has been, probably eating breakfast." I laughed and said, "Right on." They got dressed and ready to go to breakfast.

They asked me to join them so I went downstairs with them. While they ate breakfast I had a cup of tea. After breakfast we strolled around the town and the guys filled me in on all of the buildings. Then we strolled through the capital park checking out the antique show and all of the artists' works.

Then we went west on Gurley Street a couple of blocks to the Sharlot Hall Museum. The original four dwellings were completely intact. There were people dressed in late 1800 apparel acting as the folks who actually lived in the homes. They showed us all of the rooms and explained life in the earlier days. It was a very informative tour.

By then it was noon and we headed to the Palace to visit with Bill Campbell the bartender. Sure enough, when we entered the saloon there was our favorite bartender already on duty. We sat at one of the Faro tables next to the safe. He started out by telling me that the very chair that I sat in was at one time occupied by none other than Wyatt Earp.

Bill told us that Wyatt ran the Faro table at the Palace for about a year while his brother Virgil, ran a saw mill just about a mile down the road west on Gurley street. Faro was one of the most popular games in the old west, also known as "Bucking the Tiger".

Faro is a bank game, meaning that the dealer is the bank against which any number of punters bet. The players are called punters. Faro must be played on a gaming layout made up of the suit of spades. The punters use the layout to place their bets. A counter, chip or cash, is placed directly on a card painted on the layout. It is a bet that this numbered card will be the next winning card dealt. If a copper is placed on the top of the chips bet then the player is betting that this card will be dealt as a losing card.

The players can also bet on the winning card being a higher or lower denomination than the losing card by placing a counter or copper on the High Card bar. The cards are shuffled and placed in a dealing box, from which they can be withdrawn only one at a time. The top of this box is open and the face of the top card can be seen. This card is called the soda card.

The dealer pulls out the soda card and it is laid aside. The next card pulled is the losing card for the betters and it is placed on the table next to the box. The card showing in the box wins for those who have bet on it and is also the new soda card. The suit of the cards is of no consequence. The bet is on the denomination of the card.

The banker pays even money on all bets except the last turn. When only three cards remain, they must fall in one of six ways. The bank pays four to one if the punter can call the turn of the cards. That is to say, if the player can correctly predict in which order the cards will be dealt. If two of the remaining cards are the same number, called a cat hop, the bank pays two to one if the punter correctly bets the deal.

A box with a miniature layout and four beads per card was said to keep track of the cards that had been played. This was important not only for playing the call of the turn, but you did not want to place a bet on a dead card, when all four had been dealt. If you unknowingly placed your bet on a dead card and did not remove it before the dealer's last call, you lost your money to the bank or to any other player quick enough to notice your error. This game had the odds in favor of the house but the house needed a very quick and intelligent dealer.

Bill proceeded to tell us that the Palace was a popular hangout for Doc Holliday. He said that Doc did not get along real well with Virgil Earp. Doc said Virgil was not a good gambler and he would beat him on a regular basis. Doc told Bill's father Bill Senior, that Virgil just kept coming back for more even though Doc would try to talk him out of playing cards with him. Doc beat him regularly.

Virgil did not like Doc due to Doc's sordid background and his reputation being a cold killer. Virgil knew that Doc and Wyatt were friends so he kept his feelings to himself. But once in a while, the anger would come out and usually after Virgil lost at poker.

I asked him how he knew all of this history about these different old west characters. He told me that he was named after his father Bill Campbell Senior, who also was a bartender at the Palace at the time that all of this action was actually happening. Everyone called him Senior. He said that his father would come home and tell stories to him and the rest of the family. He said heck there wasn't anything else to do in those days.

Bill told me to ask any questions because there were probably hundreds of them going through my mind. He was right. My head was full of questions. He asked me if I had ever heard of Arizona Charlie, or Abram Meadows. I told him that I had no idea who this person was and that I had never heard of him. Bill then told us that Arizona Charlie was one of the most amazing old west characters and that he simply was overlooked in Arizona History.

Bill said that Arizona Charlie was born in a snowstorm in a wagon train headed from St Joseph's, Missouri to Visalia, California. Bill went on to say that Charlie grew to be six foot six inches tall and about two hundred ten pounds. He was a very big man for the old west. Most folks were five foot to six foot tall and not all that heavy. Charlie had long dark brown hair and sported mustache and goatee. He moved from Visalia to Payson because his family had gotten out of the cattle business and all he knew was being a cowboy.

Arizona Charlie was great with a rope and was able to do tricks. He was also a gambler and supposedly was good with his guns. He was a very handsome man, which was also very rare for a cowboy. He had done a little mining and won the first rodeo in Payson. Anyway, Bill went on to say that he would fill us in on Arizona Charlie a little later with regard as to how his father first met Charlie.

Bill went on to tell us that some of the local businessmen would meet every Friday after dinner to have a friendly game of poker which would usually last that evening and sometimes they would come back that next Saturday evening to finish up the game just depending on how they felt. They were all pretty well to do and most of them were not hurting for money.

The word spread about the game and one Thursday night in about October of 1886, Doc wandered into the Palace. He sat at the bar and ordered a bottle of whiskey and a shot glass and proceeded to get tanked. Bill's dad, who we'll just refer to as Senior, was the bartender on duty that night.

He knew Doc and asked him the whereabouts of Kate. Doc told Senior that Kate and Doc had a huge argument after the OK Corral incident. He said that Kate took off for Colorado and he had not seen her in four years. He said they had fought before but this was the longest time that they had been apart. Senior then asked him what he was doing in town and Doc told him that he heard that there was a good poker game every Friday night and had hoped to be able to join the game.

Bill said that Doc had slipped his father a twenty dollar bill and asked him to see if he could get him into the game. Bill's dad told him no problem. Doc wanted to know if these were the same men that he gambled with in 1880 some six years before when he left Prescott with $43,000.00. Senior looked at Doc and said, "I had no idea that you had won that much."

Senior told him that those folks were either local gamblers or visiting gamblers and that they were all gone. He told Doc that these folks were local businessmen and that the stakes were not anywhere near the big games of the past. Senior told Doc that big gambling games were long gone. Doc told Bill Senior that he had a way of bringing people down to the gutter. Senior laughed and then asked about the warrant out for his arrest.

Doc told Bill's father, "Actually, it all stemmed from the killing of Curly Bill Brosius, Frank Stillwell, and all of the rest of the Cowboys. Texas Jack, Wyatt Earp, Warren Earp, Charlie McMasters and I ended up wanted for the murder of the Cowboys, so we all took off in different directions until it all died down. It was okay for them to kill Morgan Earp in cold blood, but we were just supposed to let them get away with it all."

Doc said they had the sheriff of Tombstone, Johnny Behan, on the payroll but they were the law. He said he went looking for Kate but ended up in Glenwood Springs for his tuberculosis. He told Bill that he opened his own bar in Glenwood Springs so he could gamble, and it would be legal since he was the owner. He said they had some crazy rule that

10

the town had adopted, sort of like Whiskey Row right here in Prescott.

Doc said he knew his days were numbered with the spread of his tuberculosis, and that he was pretty uncomfortable most all of the time and had a great deal of pain in his lungs. He told Senior that it would be okay if he just did not have to breathe. He also said that he had a Yavapai Indian medicine man that had some herbs that would help him and that he had seen him yesterday on his way into town. He said that he felt better and was ready to gamble.

In any event, the governor of Arizona had given them all a full pardon after a three year investigation, and found them all innocent of murder. They were no longer trying to extradite them all back to Arizona for arrest and trial, so Doc figured he would kill two birds with one stone. Get the herbs he needed for the body and a little poker for the soul. Senior laughed and told him that he would put in a good word.

Then Doc proceeded to tell him that he was on the run from Colorado because he had a gunfight in Leadville on his way down here with a couple of old enemies, Billy Allen and Johnny Tyler, from Tombstone. Doc told Senior that he was in Leadville gambling and tended bar at Hyman's Saloon. He had borrowed five dollars from Billy Allen six months earlier in Tombstone and told him that as soon as one of the other cowboys paid him back that he had every intention of paying back Billy.

Doc said that he heard that if he did not pay Billy the five dollars, that Billy was going to find Doc and get his five dollars worth out of Doc's hide. Doc, now weighing no more than 120 lbs. looked like he had been eaten up from tuberculosis. Doc sat at the end of the bar in Hyman's saloon and waited for them to come in since they were bragging around town that they were going to gun him down. When Billy walked in the saloon, Doc shot Billy in the arm. Johnny ran out of the saloon. Somebody grabbed the gun out of Doc's hand and he was taken into custody by the town sheriff. He told the sheriff that Billy came in waving a gun. The sheriff went back to the saloon and it was discovered that Billy Allen in fact did not have a gun. Doc told Senior that he told the Judge at the trial, "Judge, look at me, I weigh no more than 120 lbs and am not in very good shape. Billy weighed around 180 and would have tossed me around the bar like an old wet hen, so I shot him."

The verdict was innocent by self-defense. Doc was escorted out of town. Doc told Senior that he headed back to Glenwood Springs for treatment for his Tuberculosis and when he felt better, he headed to Prescott. He told Senior that he knew that he would get an honest game, if he was allowed to gamble at the Palace. He told Senior that he rode the train from Colorado and was very thankful that it came right into Prescott. He said he simply did not have the energy to ride a horse all of the way from Colorado. He said the days of sleeping on the hard ground were over. He was able to rest on the train and eat good meals.

He finished the bottle and said he was headed for the St. Michael's. He was drunk enough and had enough laudanum, which is a mixture of opium and alcohol. Bill's dad told him it was a good thing he was a licensed dentist so that he could get the laudanum. He told Bill that luck had nothing to do with it, that he earned the dentist degree, but luck had a lot to do with the fact that he ended up with this death sentence disease, tuberculosis.

He said that his life style definitely did not help the cure of the disease that had stricken him. He could sleep he would just pass out. He said he would be back that Friday night and hoped to be in the game. Bill's dad said goodnight and off Doc went for the night.

Bill was telling us how his dad told him that Doc was really a pretty nice fellow. He was about 6'0" and weighed about 125 lbs and did not look good at that time. He told his family that Doc was grey in color. He said that the one thing that pissed Doc off was someone cheating at cards or not following the rules. He would always warn the other person and if the person did not listen, then things got out of hand. Doc was like a Jeckle and Hyde. He was fine until he lost his temper and then "Look out!" He was a cold-blooded killer once he lost his southern gentleman's temper, and at that point it was best to stay out of his way.

Chapter Three
Telling the Family

Senior then told his son, Bill Junior, that the next day, Friday, at about 10:00 a.m., a stranger came in the bar. Looking dusty from a long ride, he asked for a cold beer. He was an ornery looking sort of fellow, about 5'9" tall and weighed about 175 lbs. He was a stout looking man with large arms and shoulders. He did not look like he had an ounce of fat on him. He was a little balding on the top and the hair he had left was black. He also had piercing dark brown eyes.

He was definitely a mean looking character. He carried what looked like a Sharps rifle in a beautiful leather sheath and was packing a Colt peacemaker on his right side. He had army pants on and an old army hat. He was not exactly dressed for a party. He asked if there was a place around where he could get a room to bathe and clean up. Bill Senior said he could go right down the street to the St Michael's Hotel and get a room.

After he had another beer the stranger asked Bill Senior about the Poker game. Senior, the bartender, asked him how he heard about the game. Tom said he'd just gotten his discharge papers from the Army in Bisbee. He told us he was one of the army scouts that helped to capture Geronimo. He said that he stopped in Tombstone looking for a friendly game of Poker and one of the dealers told him about a game that is played every Friday evening at the Palace Saloon in Prescott.

He said after the dusty ride he needed a bath and some new clothes and he had hoped to join in the poker game to relax since he had been chasing Geronimo for over three years. He introduced himself as "Tom Horn." Senior said he had heard of him and everybody was glad that Geronimo was captured. He was sure they would be happy to let him in

14

the game. He then left for the hotel and said he would be back in hopes of getting in the game at 7:00 that Friday evening.

Bill Senior then told his son that at about 5:00 pm the regulars started showing up for the game. There were four players who were local businessmen William Claypool, George Waddell, Ed Horne and Doug Aitken. They all arrived within a couple of minutes of each other. They took their regular table next to the north wall across from the bar, and right next to the safe that was built in the wall. It was the larger table and was round and Bill Senior always reserved the table just for them. They sat down and each ordered a libation and asked Bill Senior to bring them a new deck of cards.

This was one of the highlights of the Palace Saloon. New decks of cards were always available. This was one of the calling cards of the Palace - a new deck anytime a customer wanted one. Bill told us the owner had a storeroom that was full of new decks of cards printed with the Palace Saloon name. This was a friendly game of five-card draw and they played it straight up, nothing wild. They had a $25 ante and no more than $25 per raise. They did play jacks or better to open but the dealer had to declare the rule before dealing the cards. They played Stud Poker, but only on occasion. Generally it was straight five-card draw.

They started early that evening and were in full swing by six pm. George Waddell had the biggest pile of money in that first hour, having won three pots. At about 6:30 Tom Horn arrived and stepped up to the bar and ordered a shot of whiskey and a cold beer. One of the locals, Bill Claypool, recognized him and called him by name.

Tom turned around to see who had called his name and as Bill stood up, a smile came across Tom's face. He went right over to the table and shook Bill's hand. It seems that Tom had been a regular customer several years earlier in Bill

15

Claypool's mercantile store. It had been several years since they saw each other.

Bill asked Tom where he had been hiding. Tom then told him that he had spent the past three years working for the army trying to capture Geronimo. He told Bill that they finally caught up to him in Mexico. They brought him back to the reservation for trial. Bill Claypool introduced Tom to the rest of the regulars and asked Tom if he wanted to join them in a friendly game of poker.

Tom laughed and told Bill that he actually had come in hopes of joining their game. He told Bill that their regular Friday game was known as far as Tombstone. Bill laughed and Ed told him that it was only known because the owner of the Bird Cage had a bar in Tombstone as well as here in Prescott. They told Tom about all of the rules and he said that he could live with the rules. He was just looking for a little excitement and the dollar amount was not that important.

He pulled up a chair and was in the next hand. George Waddell started losing and was a little antsy. Bill Claypool told him that sometimes when others join the game, the luck changes due to the positioning of the cards from four players to five players. Everything was going fine until just before 8:00 pm. That is when Doc walked through the doors and entered the saloon. Actually none of the regulars recognized Doc, and Tom had his back to the entrance so he did not see Doc walk in. Doc strolled up to the bar and ordered his usual bottle of Jack Daniels. Why not? He was a southerner and this was his drink.

After the next hour of gambling they had a new leader, local Ed Horne. Bill Senior brought over another round of drinks and before they could pay he told them that the gentleman at the bar bought the round and had hoped to join the game. They all turned and looked to the bar and Doc turned and waved to them.

Tom waved. He was the only one that recognized Doc. He told the regulars that he knew the guy and excused himself for a minute while he went over to see Doc. They shook hands and Tom told Doc that he was surprised to see him and that he had heard that Doc's health was really failing. Doc informed Tom that his health had been shit for several years and it was true, he was definitely not getting any better. Tom told Doc that the game was probably not going to get the blood flowing for a gambler of his stature. Doc told Tom that he could not understand what had happened in the Poker world but that there were simply no big games around anymore.

After Tom told him the rules, Doc told Tom that he could live with the local's rules. Tom brought Doc over to the table and asked his friends if Doc could join them. The regulars told Tom that any friend of his was a friend of theirs and that this Doc guy was welcome to join. Tom told them that he had explained the rules. The only one to complain was Ed. What a surprise - he was winning.

Doc pulled up a chair and joined the game. It was about 9:00 p.m. and the game was going well. It appeared that Doc was up and a couple of the regulars were down. Just then, the Sheriff arrived and walked up to the table. He waited until they had finished the hand and then he spoke directly to Doc. He told Doc that he knew that he was in town and wanted to know his intentions.

Doc told the sheriff that he was not looking for any trouble and that he just wanted a friendly game of poker. The Sheriff told him that he did not believe that Doc knew a friendly game existed. He informed Doc that he did not want any trouble and that trouble simply followed Doc Holliday everywhere he went. The regulars' lower jaws dropped when they heard the name Doc Holliday. They looked at Tom and addressed him saying that they knew who Doc was and should not have let a professional gambler and killer join their game. Tom told them all that Doc was a gentleman and that when playing with gentlemen that he would be a gentleman.

Doc interrupted and explained that, yes, he had a reputation. He said that in his profession one runs into a lot of low life individuals and that he had enough of those types of people. He told them that his disease was eating him up and that he did not have long to live. He had hoped that they would just allow him the pleasure of a good poker game.

He told them that he could live with their rules and there was no need to fear him when among gentlemen. He considered it an honor to be allowed to play in their game and he respected them. Ed said, "Sounds good to me. You have been a perfect gentleman, and now let's play poker." They thanked the sheriff and Ed dealt the cards for the next hand. Ironically, Doc won the next hand.

It was about 11:00 p.m. when the local four players decided to call it a night. Doc, Tom, and Bill Claypool were up but not more than a couple hundred a piece. Ed, George, and Doug Aitken were down with Ed being the big loser, having lost $300. He did not seem upset. He said that it had been a fun night and the locals had something to talk about, gambling with the likes of Doc Holliday and Tom Horn.

Ed went on to say that he would be back Saturday evening if Tom and Doc were going to be around for another evening of gambling. They both told him that they had come to play poker and they would be right here in this spot the next night. Doc said that they would be ready for another game at 8:00 tomorrow, Saturday night. Tom and Doc stayed for another hour playing and then Doc called it quits.

Senior told his son, Bill Jr., that neither said much so he did not know who had won or lost. He said that they were both very quiet and reserved. They came up to the bar and had one last shot before heading to the hotel. It was hard to believe that two such notorious old west characters could be in one spot and that there was not one incident or hot shot pistolero to interrupt the evening.

As they were leaving, Senior heard Doc tell Tom that this was one of best evenings that he had ever spent gambling. He told Tom that he wished that his whole life had gone this smoothly. Tom piped up and said that if it had gone like this evening that Doc would have had a very meager existence and would not have been able to enjoy his crazy outlandish lifestyle.

Chapter Four
Ready for the Game

The next day, Saturday, was another cold brisk day. Senior told his son that he arrived at the bar at 10:00 a.m. and opened for business. Several locals came in and there was a lot of talk about the game of the night before. They all asked Senior if it was true that Doc Holliday and Tom Horn were actually gambling here last night.

Senior told them all it was an uneventful evening and that the game went well. No incidents of violence at all. They were all in complete shock. They asked if the men had left town. Senior told them that they were planning another evening of gambling that very night. The locals finished their drinks and bolted out of the saloon.

Bill Senior knew that this night would be action packed for sure. It was only 10:30 a.m. and he knew that the word would spread about Doc and Tom being in town. Having both of these notorious men in town was definitely big local news and they could not expect another uneventful evening. The saloon started to fill up by 4:00 p.m. and by 6:00 p.m. the saloon was packed in anticipation of the big game.

The first to arrive was Tom Horn. He made his way through the crowd to their reserved table. Senior came over and brought him a cold beer. Senior told Ed that the place started to fill up at 4:00 pm in anticipation of the game. Bill went on to say that there was no way that they could keep the presence of both Doc and Tom quiet in such a small town. He said that the sheriff had plans to stay the entire evening while the game was being played.

Sure enough, Doc rolled in about 15 minutes later between six-thirty and seven o'clock. He moved to the table and took his seat. Doc looked at Tom and said that he had never played in the presence of such a huge crowd for such small stakes. Ed laughed and told them both that he had never played to such a crowd in his entire life. Ed told Doc and Tom he had never been a celebrity. Doc said he hoped that this was the extent of the excitement.

Bill Senior brought over a bottle of Jack Daniels and three glasses. He told Ed and Tom that Doc was buying for his friends for the evening and that was all that was to be said. He told Ed and Tom that he still had a lot of southern hospitality. Bill brought along two new fresh decks of cards. Doc told Ed to do the honors and open the deck and pass it around to Tom to inspect.

Tom and Doc asked Ed if he came prepared for a real game and told Ed that he and Tom had decided to up the stakes to a $25 ante and $50 per raise. Ed told them that he actually expected the game to change and that he came prepared. The games went well back and forth. Each player had won several hands and it looked like there was no real big winner.

Then at about 10:00 pm, Ed got up and said that he was broke and had lost all he was going to lose. He finished his shot of whiskey and shook hands with both Tom and Doc and made his way out through the crowd. He shook hands with many of the folks that were in the crowd. Even though he lost $3,000 he felt honored to have played with Tom and Doc. Doc looked at Tom and said that without another player joining them that their game was just about over.

Tom spoke out loud and asked if anyone wanted to join the game. They heard a voice come from the Bar and the person said, "I would like to join you." Doc called out, "Come over." This very tall man, who was at least 6'6", weighing well over 200 lbs, with long black hair and a mustache, strolled up to the table. He was dressed very sharply with a long cowhide leather jacket with fringe hanging down in the middle and at the bottom. It looked like it had been made by Indians. In fact, Tom mentioned that he liked the jacket. The stranger put his hand out and introduced himself as Abram Meadows, also known as Arizona Charlie.

Tom smiled because he knew Charlie from the local rodeos. He and Charlie went head to head on many occasions at the Payson Rodeo, and several small Arizona town rodeos and usually it came down to one of them. Charlie told them he got the jacket from a Yavapai Indian chief in a trade. He had two pistols in holsters in front of his hips, strangely enough, with the butts of the guns facing each other.

Doc stood up first and introduced himself. Doc looked at the stranger and said, "You must have been the tallest one in your school." Charlie responded by laughing and saying, "Not only was I the tallest in the school, but I was the tallest in the whole town of Visalia, California." Doc thought to himself that he had never seen anyone wear his guns in such a strange manner, with only the buckle separating the holsters. He was also a little impressed when he saw that this stranger had a knife hanging in a sheath on his right hip.

Doc was intrigued looking at the knife. Doc had become an expert with a knife and he had not before seen anyone packing a knife in a sheath. The stranger was a little taken aback and made the comment that he had heard of Doc Holliday and was happy to have finally had the chance to meet him in person. Tom stood up and Doc introduced Tom to Charlie.

Charlie said immediately that he had heard of Tom and commented that he heard Tom was involved in the capture of Geronimo. Tom said "Yep that is me, the same person." Doc had immediately noticed the position of Charlie's guns and made a comment. Charlie simply told him that it was a free country and that this was the best way for him to carry the weapons. Doc laughed. Doc thought to himself that there was no way this guy could draw with any speed with the weapons positioned the way Charlie had them.

Doc was an expert at sizing up his playing partners because, with his experience, after a person had a couple of drinks, the alcohol would give them liquid courage. He was always looking for an edge. After over twenty years as a gambler, the only thing that would keep him gambling was a fight. This guy Arizona Charlie was a fancy looking dude and Doc just thought this guy was another imitator.

Doc mentioned he had never seen guns that small and asked Charlie what caliber they were. Charlie said they were specially built nickel plated 1849 Colt Pocket Model Pistols that were 31 caliber and that the pistols were made to his specifications. Tom said he had never seen a more stunning set of pistols, but he said a 35 caliber pistol was like a pea shooter compared to the 45 caliber Peacemaker. Charlie simply said that he could hit the target.

Charlie mentioned that he was just looking for a friendly game of poker and was not looking for any trouble. Doc laughed and said that this was a friendly game and went on to explain the rules. Doc said that he never looked for trouble and that in most circumstances in the past, the other gamblers got out of hand. He said that he was always able to control his alcohol but that he had never met anyone else that had the ability to keep a cool mind in the heat of battle.

Doc told Charlie that he and Tom and several of the locals had gambled the night before with no incidents. He had hoped this evening would go smoothly. Charlie told them both that he had come prepared financially to gamble and did not plan to loose the game or his temper. He said that he had respect for both of them and that he hoped the evening would go smoothly.

Chapter Five
The Game Begins

Doc yelled to Senior to bring over a couple of new decks of cards and another round of drinks for themselves and their new friend Charlie, and he put the drinks on his tab. Senior brought over two shots of Jack Daniels and one shot of Tequila. He brought them a beer chaser along with the shot. Charlie immediately said thank you.

Doc handed the cards to Charlie and told him to cut the cards and pick a card, and then handed the deck to Tom so he could pick a card, then lastly Doc picked a card. The highest card picked would deal the first hand. Tom drew an Ace, so he got the deal. They each put up their respective ante, which had now been bumped to $50, and Tom dealt out five cards to each of them. He called this game five card draw, nothing wild.

Doc was to the left of Charlie so he was given the first opportunity. Doc pondered his cards for about two minutes and asked for two cards and discarded two. Charlie was next and he also took two cards and discarded two cards. Last but not least, it was Tom's turn and he took two cards and discarded two cards. Doc was then given the opportunity to place his first bet. He bet $50, which was the maximum bet. The bet then went to Charlie who raised the stakes another $50, bringing the bet to Tom, who promptly raised the stakes another $50.

The bet now was back to Doc and he put up $100 to make the pot right. They had all agreed to two rounds of betting so now Charlie bet another $25, and Tom passed the raise to Doc, who immediately bumped the raise to an additional $50. He turned to Charlie and said, "It is $75 to you, where do you stand?" Charlie immediately put out the $75. It was up to Tom now whether he would stay.

Tom bet the maximum $50, no raises, then both Doc and Charlie matched the bet, and now it was showtime. Doc threw down a pair of aces. Tom threw down a pair of queens.

Arizona Charlie. Photo courtesy of Sharlott Hall Museum.

Charlie threw down a straight and that was the winning hand. Charlie was excited that he had won a $600 pot. Since he won the hand, it was his turn to deal.

Charlie called for seven card stud, no peek, with the first two down and dirty. That meant that the first two cards were not to be looked at and the other five cards were to be dealt face up. The highest card placed the first bet, and then the highest hand bet with each card dealt until the five were dealt. There would be betting with each card and a final bet with the last two cards. The winner would be determined by choosing his best five cards out of the seven that would be dealt to each player.

Charlie dealt two cards each to Tom and Doc and two to himself. Those two cards were the down and dirty. The next card dealt would be the up card. He dealt Doc the Ace of Hearts and then Tom was dealt the Ace of Spades. Charlie dealt himself a Ten of Spades. The Ace of Spades is the highest card so Tom placed the first bet, which was $50. Doc matched the bet but did not raise the bet. Charlie just had to stay in the game. Even though he only had a ten showing, he had no idea what cards were the down cards. There were still five cards yet to come, so he placed his bet to match $50.

Charlie started to think to himself that he was really gambling with two cool characters. There was no way to read either of them. It was too early anyway. He felt like he was the student amidst these two professional gamblers. The next card that was dealt to Doc was a queen of diamonds and then Charlie dealt Tom the six of clubs. His card was the jack of diamonds. High hand now showing was Doc's ace and queen.

Doc opened with $50 and Tom and Charlie matched the bet but no raises. The next card dealt to Doc was the five of hearts. Then Charlie dealt Tom the six of diamonds and finally he dealt himself the queen of clubs. Tom, with a pair of sixes was the high hand, and he bet $100. Doc and Charlie matched the pot but made no raises. Charlie then dealt Doc the ace of clubs. He dealt Tom the five of spades and himself the jack of spades.

At this point Doc, with the pair of aces showing, was the highest hand and he bet $100. Tom passed the bet and Charlie raised Doc's bet by $50. Tom matched the bet to stay in at least for the last card. Besides, they had no idea what cards were down and dirty. The adrenaline was flowing. Charlie then dealt the last card to each.

He dealt the four of diamonds to Doc, the king of hearts to Tom, and finally, the nine of diamonds to himself. Doc was still the high hand with the pair of aces. He immediately bet $100 and Tom bumped the bet $50 to $150 then passed the bet to Charlie. Charlie bumped the bet another $50 bringing his total to $200 to make the pot right. Doc and Tom both put in their additional monies to match the pot.

Since Charlie had the lowest hand, he showed his down cards. He had the nine and eight of clubs. His best five cards were a straight. Charlie immediately bet $100 and both Tom and Doc matched the pot. Tom showed his down cards, which were the six of spades and the three of clubs. He had three sixes, but Charlie still had the high hand. He bet another $100, and at that point Tom dropped out. Doc stayed and matched the pot and bumped the pot another $50 bringing his bet to $150.

Doc flipped over his cards and showed the seven of diamonds and the queen of hearts. He had two pair. Charlie with the straight was the winning hand. He just smiled and raked in the cash. He was very surprised but very happy. This was the biggest pot of the night. He had won the first two hands and he was excited.

Chapter Six
Hot under the Collar

There was not much time to enjoy the winning hand. Bill Senior brought another round of drinks to the table and Tom told Bill that this round was on Charlie. Charlie laughed and said he would be happy to buy the round. Charlie dealt the next hand and went with the standard five card draw straight up, which means nothing is wild. Doc won the hand and the $600 pot with three aces.

Doc dealt the next hand and continued with five card draw, which was his signature game and ironically, he won the next hand and pot of $800 with two pair, queens and sixes. Charlie and Doc could see that Tom was getting frustrated. He stroked his moustache. Nobody said a word. Charlie and Doc felt his pain because they had been there before on a losing streak. Doc had no habits that would give away his position. Charlie simply sat with his left hand placed on his left thigh.

Doc dealt the next hand of five card draw and Tom ended up winning a pot worth $1,100 with a full house, queens over eights. Charlie noticed that Tom seemed more relieved than happy about the win. Tom dealt the next hand, which was a game of five card draw. Doc ended up winning the hand with a King high straight and took the $750 pot.

After that game they took a break and Doc and Tom went out back to the outhouse and Charlie went to the bar for another shot. There were several folks at the bar and they started talking to Charlie. He told them that frankly he was happy to be holding his own with both Doc and Tom. Senior heard him admit to one of the locals that he could not imagine that he would ever be playing with both of them.

Tom and Doc came up to the bar and Charlie immediately bought them a drink. They all leaned against the bar and discussed the evening. Doc mentioned that he had never seen a man carry his guns the way Charlie wore his pistols. Charlie explained that the position of his holsters was just the way that he taught himself how to draw. Doc said it seemed that it would be faster to draw from the hip, as that is where your arm and hand are placed to be the most efficient.

Charlie told Doc that everything he said made perfect sense but he defended his position by simply saying that he could hold his own. Doc laughed and said to Charlie that it looked like the placement of the guns would impede him when urinating. Charlie said that since he was so tall that the holsters did not get in the way. He said, "Come on with me and I will show you." All three of them broke out laughing. Tom said, "Let's get on with it. I am down and need a chance to get even."

By this time it was eleven o'clock. The bar was still packed. It was like they were in a gallery waiting for something to happen. Doc dealt the first hand of the second round and Tom ended up winning the hand with a pair of tens. The pot was $850. Tom then called seven-card stud as his choice of game, straight up with the best five cards as the hand to be played. Charlie could see that Tom was a little aggravated.

Tom said that he wanted a chance to get even and this would be a big pot. They decided to bump the ante to $100 and bumped the bets to $100 but stayed with three raises per card. Charlie dealt the first two cards to each player and they were the down cards. The first up card was dealt to Doc, which was a four of diamonds. He dealt Tom the queen of hearts, and he dealt himself the three of clubs.

Tom was the high card and bet $100. The bet passed to Charlie. He matched the bet and then the bet passed to Doc who matched the pot. Nobody raised Tom's bet. Charlie dealt the next card to Doc, which was the king of hearts. He dealt Tom the ten of clubs and dealt himself the eight of clubs. Doc was the high hand with the king and four showing. He bet $100. The bet then passed to Tom with the queen and ten showing. He matched Doc's $100 and bumped the bet another $100.

With the eight and three of clubs showing, Charlie had to think a little, but decided to stay in the game because there were three more cards yet to be dealt. He threw in his $200 and then passed the bet to Doc who matched the pot with $100. He did not bump the bet. Charlie dealt Doc the ten of diamonds and then dealt Tom the ace of diamonds and dealt himself the three of spades. Charlie now had the high hand showing with the pair of threes. He immediately bet $100.

Doc was next with the king, ten, and four showing. He knew that it was still early so he matched the bet. Tom was next and bumped the bet to another $100. Charlie and Doc matched the pot but no raises. Charlie dealt the next card to Doc, which was the king of diamonds. To Tom he dealt the deuce of clubs and to himself he dealt the king of clubs. Doc, now with the pair of kings was the high hand and bet $100.

Tom pondered because he did not have much showing but he still had two down cards. So he matched the pot and passed the bet to Charlie who matched the pot and raised the bet by another $100 because he had a pair of threes showing. He pondered what he had as down cards. Doc matched the bet and passed to Tom. Tom, with just nothing showing, looked a little upset but threw in his hundred to make the pot right.

Charlie dealt the last card to each player and dealt Doc the ten of spades. He then dealt Tom the ace of hearts and finally dealt himself the three of diamonds. Charlie, now with three threes showing, had the high hand and bet $100. Doc matched the pot because he only had a pair of tens showing. Tom stayed in reluctantly with his pair of aces but again he was not sure what was down.

Charlie raised the bet by another $100 and why not? He had three of a kind showing. Doc matched the pot and Tom grumbled, but knew that he had to stay in at this point, so he matched the pot. Doc turned his down cards up first and they were the seven of spades and the eight of hearts. His best five cards ended up being two pair of kings over tens. Tom went next. He turned up a four of clubs and the five of diamonds. Tom, holding just the pair of aces, threw his cards into the discard pile.

The hand was over. Charlie won the hand with three of a kind showing. Tom asked him to show the down cards. Charlie did not have to but he obliged because he was also curious as it turned out he had the king of spades and the seven of hearts. He ended up with a full house. The pot was the biggest of the night… $3,200.

Tom rose from his chair and slammed a shot of tequila. He looked right at Charlie and then looked over at Doc and said to Doc, "You know Doc, this guy has kicked our ass tonight and I do not know how he is cheating. Nobody can be that lucky." Doc looked back at Tom and said that he thought this guy was simply lucky. He told Tom that he could not see any traits that would indicate that Charlie had been cheating. Tom just got more upset and looked right at Charlie and accused him of cheating.

Charlie stood up and looked right at Tom and said that he felt bad that Tom had been the big loser that evening but that he was not cheating and took offense to the remark. Tom said, "Do you want to do it right here?" and Charlie said, "No, I want to take it out front. If I am to die I want to die in the street. No sense in taking any other lives with this crowd around."

Chapter Seven
Time for Action

Charlie, Tom, and Doc stood up and made their way through the crowd. As they passed the bar, Charlie turned to Bill Senior and asked him to come out from behind the bar and bring two shot glasses with him. The crowd had already cleared out of the bar and was in the street waiting in great anticipation. Tom told Charlie that the drinking was over and it was time for shooting.

Charlie looked at Tom and said, "Can you indulge a doomed person?" Tom said, "Sure go right ahead." and waved Charlie forward. When they got to the street, Charlie asked Tom if he could show them something before somebody died. Tom said, "It is time for shooting." Doc looked over and said to Tom, "What do you have to lose? This guy is probably going to die so let him have his fun, then we will split his winnings."

Charlie told Bill to go out in the street about thirty feet. Bill went to the middle of the street and turned to face the guys. Tom yelled, "Let's get on with this!" Charlie told Bill to throw both of the shot glasses straight up into the night sky as far as he could. Bill threw them up and Charlie drew both pistols and shot both glasses out of the air with one bullet from each pistol.

Doc's lower lip dropped and then Charlie turned to Tom and said, "Do you still want to get it on?" Tom looked very stunned. He was great with a rifle, especially a fifty caliber Sharps, but this guy was one of the best shots with a pistol that he had ever seen. He patted Charlie on the back and said, "No, I think I will just apologize if that is acceptable to you." He then patted Charlie on the back and said to Charlie and Doc, "Let's go back into the bar and I will buy all of us a round of drinks."

They all strolled up to the Bar and Bill Senior poured all of them a shot of Jack Daniels and a mug of beer. Bill, told them the drinks were on the house. He said, "he had never seen a display of shooting like that in his entire life." Doc looked right at Bill and said," Bill, you are right." I have never seen anybody that fast with such amazing accuracy." Doc slammed the shot of Jack Daniels, looked at Bill and said he was damn glad that Charlie wasn't in Tombstone at the time of the big gunfight at the OK Corral the results may have been very different. Doc turned to Charlie and asked him why nobody knew him. Charlie told them both that after he displays his ability that the fight usually never happens. Doc told them that he knew that there was nobody any better with a rifle than Tom Horn. "But I have to tell you, Tom," said Doc, "that I have never seen anybody with the speed and accuracy of Arizona Charlie."

Tom looked over at Charlie and thanked him for the shooting display. He said that he would rather lose a few thousand dollars than lose his life. They all slammed another shot and Doc asked Charlie if he could see his guns.

Charlie pulled both guns and gave one to each of them to look at. Doc commented that the caliber of his pistols was not 45. He said that most gunfighters who are accurate are not usually fast because they pack the big 45 caliber peacemaker. It is very hard to pull such a heavy pistol and be fast.

He went on to say that even though his pistols were smaller in size, weight, and caliber, what counted was the end result. Tom asked Charlie if he had ever killed anybody. Charlie told him that he had never shot anybody. The disagreement always ended after his demonstration. He told them that during the day he has someone throw up two silver dollars.

He went on to say that at night he went with the shot glasses because the silver dollars are just too hard to see in the dark. Charlie said that he really did not want to kill anybody but that he was not afraid to die. Tom told him that there was no sense talking anymore. He told Doc that it did not matter. Tom told Doc that he had seen all he needed and that he was not willing to draw against Charlie.

Chapter Eight
Returning from the Street

They all had another shot and a beer. Doc, being very proficient with a knife, could not refrain from asking Charlie if he was as good with the knife as he was with his guns. Charlie told them both that had done a little buffalo hunting and learned to be mule-skinner out of necessity. Tom asked about the guns.

Charlie told Tom that he had them specially built to his specifications. He said that he wanted a shorter barrel on his model so as not to interfere with his thigh action. He was not going to change the way he had learned to draw. The positioning of the pistols still allowed him to pack the knife on his right hip. Charlie told them that the guns were also perfectly balanced. Doc and Tom said they had never heard of perfectly balanced guns and they wanted to know what being balanced meant. Charlie told them to step back and he would show them.

Charlie pulled both pistols from the holster and proceeded to give them a tremendous display of speed and hand coordination by spinning the pistols in all directions and both in perfect harmony. The demonstration lasted several minutes. After spinning the pistols, he holstered them just as quickly as he had drawn them.

Doc mentioned that the only person that he ever saw with similar dexterity was Johnny Ringo, but he could only do the spinning display with one hand. Charlie said that he had a lot of practice, but the fact that the pistols were perfectly balanced made it easier to learn. Doc asked if he could see one of the pistols again and in no time he was spinning the pistol with the same level of hand coordination as Charlie. Doc told them both that his career as a gambler would have gone a lot smoother had he had balanced pistols.

Charlie told them it was never too late. Charlie told them that the gunsmith actually lived right there in Prescott and he would be happy to fix each of them up with the same balanced pistols. He told them that good equipment made all the difference in his skill level. Doc just could not hold back anymore. He asked Charlie about the knife and if he was proficient with it.

Charlie, not being a showoff but having had enough drinks under his belt, pointed to a poster on the north wall across from the bar over the gambling tables and right next to the wall safe. Doc and Tom looked up, and right at that instant, Charlie drew the knife. It was like slow motion, people were walking back and forth and it seemed to stop in time. Before they could say a word, Charlie threw it between the tables, between the people standing, walking, and sitting at the tables, with lightning speed and stuck it in the middle of a poster that was about twenty feet away against the wall opposite of the bar.

Doc and Tom stood with their mouths wide open. Doc told them he thought that he himself was very proficient with a knife, but the only man he ever saw that was as good as Charlie was a Mississippi river boat gambler named Johnny Diamond. He told Charlie that to be as skillful as he was with both the guns and the knife was amazing. Charlie told them he had spent many nights practicing when he was a muleskinner. He said that he also spent many nights around a campfire as a cowboy so he had a lot of time to practice these skills with both his guns and the knife. He felt that if he could be proficient that he might never have to pull either to kill anybody.

Then Doc told both Tom and Charlie that he was glad that he did not call Charlie a cheat. Tom said he was glad he was alive to see this demonstration. They continued to party the rest of the evening and even though Charlie had won the most money, he did not buy another drink. They never continued the game, and Doc and Tom wanted to know how Charlie had become such a good gambler. Charlie smiled at both of them and said, "Down right pure luck, that is all I can say." They all headed to the St Michael's at about three in the morning and called it a night.

When Bill finished the story I looked at him in total amazement. He smiled and then said," You must have a million questions running through your head." I said, "You are right." The first question was, "How did you remember all of those facts in such detail?" Bill smiled and then said, "It is very simple. I was there in the crowd. As I said earlier, my father was the bartender and when he came home that Friday night and told us all the story, I decided that I was not about to miss the game on Saturday night. This was the biggest event to hit Prescott in my short life. I was ten years old at the time. Just about the same age you are right now." He smiled and then said, "I bet you will never forget this story yourself." I smiled at him and said, "You are right about that fact." Just then Kenny and Rudy walked up and patted me on the back. They told me it was time to head home. I turned and thanked Bill and smiled. I talked about the game all of the way home. Bill passed away about six months after our visit. He was a great guy and I really appreciated him sharing the story with me.

Chapter Nine
They Went on Their Way

Doc left Prescott five days after the big night in the Palace and headed back to Glenwood Springs to the sanatorium for treatment for his tuberculosis. But before he left he participated in several more poker games and left town with $5,000. His TB had gotten so bad that he could not even gamble for more than a couple of hours at any one time. He had his own bar in Glenwood Springs and spent his last days between his bar and the sanatorium. He passed away on November 8, 1887 in the sanatorium in Glenwood Springs, Colorado.

Tom Horn left Prescott the next day and moved to Globe where he was a ranch hand and proved to be a great cowboy. He won the World Championship Rodeo competition in Globe, Arizona in 1888. Horn joined the Pinkerton Detective Agency in 1890 and used his rifle with lethal effectiveness. He worked out of the Denver offices, chasing bank robbers and train thieves throughout Colorado and Wyoming.

Tom Horn was fearless and would face any outlaw or gunman. On one occasion, he rode into an outlaw hideout known as Hole-in-the-Wall and single handedly captured the notorious Peg-Leg Watson (alias Peg-Leg McCoy), who had recently robbed a mail train with others. Horn tracked Watson to a high mountain cabin and called out to him, telling the outlaw that he was coming in for him.

Watson stepped out from the cabin with two six guns in his hands. He watched, open-mouthed, as Horn walked resolutely toward him across an open field, his Winchester 30/30 carried limply at his side. Watson never fired a shot and Horn took him to jail without a struggle. Tom bragged that Watson did not give him much trouble during the capture.

This one arrest was so well documented that Tom Horn became a living legend. He hunted down and killed seventeen men while working for the Pinkertons. He quit and was recruited by the Wyoming Cattle Growers Association. It was his job to track down cattle rustlers and heckle and scare anybody that tried to homestead on the cattle range. He was paid $600 for each rustler and part of the job was to scare the settlers.

Horn proved to be a methodical man hunter and ruthless killer. He would spend several days tracking the rustlers, learning their habits and observing them each night. Then when he caught them in the act he would shoot them with a high powered Sharps 50 caliber at long range. After he killed them, he would put a large rock underneath their head which was his trademark that he had killed the rustler. This was to scare any other rustler and to prove that he had done the killing and to verify his reward.

His last killing was his undoing. Again, he had perfected the long distance murder. On the morning of July 18, 1901 on the Powder River near Cheyenne Wyoming, Horn lay in wait for rancher Kels P. Nickell, who had been marked for death by competing ranchers. He had only seen Nickell once from a distance, so Horn did not recognize Willie Nickell, the rancher's tall 14 year old son, who appeared that morning, driving his father's wagon out of the ranch yard.

Willie had on his father's coat and hat and when he got down from the wagon to open the gate, Horn fired a shot that struck the boy. Willie staggered to his feet and tried to get back on the wagon but Horn fired another shot striking him in the back of the head, killing him instantly. The killing was immediately attributed to Horn because of the method used.

Joe Lefors, the famous Wyoming lawman got Tom drunk in a bar and overheard Tom talk about the Nickell killing. Tom told Joe in the bar that if he had shot the boy that it would have been his greatest shot and would have been the low down worse deed that he had ever committed. He never admitted that he shot the boy. He never claimed that he did not. They were never really able to prove that Tom actually killed the boy. He claimed that he would not have missed on the first shot. Nevertheless, he was sentenced to death and was hung on November 20, 1903.

Arizona Charlie won the first Rodeo in Prescott in 1888 and over the years he and Tom Horn locked horns in many rodeo competitions. Charlie usually won most of the competitions. In 1895 Charlie put on three days of Mexican bull fighting in Cripple Creek Colorado. Bull fighting was against the law so he was promptly arrested after the bull fights commenced.

During the late 1800's and the early 1900's, Charlie became good friends with Wyatt and Josie Earp. They lived on a ranch between Mayer and Prescott and Charlie would visit them from time to time. He told them that gold had been discovered near Dawson in the Yukon Territory. He left by ship in 1897 and scaled Chilkoot Pass in sub zero weather and arrived in Dawson in December of that year.

There was a tremendous famine in Dawson. It was a typical mining boomtown like Tombstone but the difference was that there was no way to get food to the town in the bitter cold winter. When he got there in the middle of winter there were great hardships. The miners were starving and had nothing to eat or drink because it was 600 miles to Dawson City and there was no way to get food or booze across the Northwest Territories. The miners had a ton of money but nowhere to spend it so they did a lot of gambling.

Charlie, being the entrepreneur, went into business printing the Klondike News, which netted him $50,000 for the one and only issue printed. Then, in July of 1899, he opened the Grand Opera House, which provided first class entertainment and expensive champagne that went for $5 a bottle. High dollar liquor and yes, high stakes gaming.

It is said that he sent a wire to Wyatt and Josie and invited them to join him. There was a job for Wyatt as a Faro dealer, and Josie as a singer and actor. Wyatt had been dealing Faro in Mayer and Charlie knew that Wyatt was one of the best Faro dealers of the old west. The word is that they joined him and they all made a lot of money.

Charlie got bored, and in 1901 to 1903 he joined the Buffalo Bill Wild West Show and toured England. He still owned the Opera house and the word is that Wyatt and Josie ran it for him while he was gone. Charlie came back to Dawson after riding with Buffalo Bill's Wild West Show. Charlie lived the rest of his life in Dawson and he never married. He was a free spirit in every sense of the word. That is probably why he was good friends with Wyatt and Josie Earp. Arizona Charlie Meadows died at the age of eighty in 1929, just a few months after his friend Wyatt Earp passed away.

In 1900 there was a huge fire that started behind Whiskey Row. The fire moved slowly but it was obvious to the original owners of the Palace that the whole square block was in the path of the raging fire. They were able to move all of the original tables and chairs, the bar itself, and the mahogany pillars and mirrors from behind the bar. The whole interior that could be moved was moved by hand to a safe area in the town.

Sure enough the palace, as well as every other bar and business establishment south of Gurley on the west side of Montezuma, burned to the ground. When they rebuilt the bars and establishments on Whiskey Row, including the St Michael's Hotel, the owners of the Palace moved all of the items saved and restored the Palace back to the same condition that it was prior to the fire.

I was in the Palace less than a week ago and everything is just as it was when it was built in 1870. There are pictures of all the characters in this story around the bar except for one, Arizona Charlie Meadows, and I believe that his picture will be hanging in the Palace very soon. It is a very historic building and the new owners have a good menu and they usually have live music on Friday and Saturday nights.

Chapter Ten
Meeting Hessy

I was up in Prescott a couple of weeks ago to visit my mother, who now lives just down the street from Whiskey Row. It had been over forty years since old Bill told me the story about game at the Palace. I always like to stop by on the way out of town and have a cold beer and just reminisce.

I stopped in that day on the way out of town and ordered a cold beer. I walked around the establishment with my beer in hand and let my imagination run wild. They have a case set up with tourist items from the Palace right at the end of the bar. They have t-shirts, dress shirts, shot glasses, regular beer glasses and many other items. The only item missing was a deck of cards, which was their calling card in the old west.

As I looked in the case I asked the bartender why they did not have decks of cards with the Palace picture available. He said they had never heard that the cards were a calling card. Just then a little voice behind me spoke up and said, "He's right Sonny, you should be selling decks of cards." She asked me to join her.

I looked over and this lady had to be in her late 80's or early 90's. She introduced herself as Hessy. She asked me how I knew about the decks of cards. I explained that I had completed a great deal of research with regard to the Palace Bar. She said, "I bet you didn't learn everything." I smiled and said, "No way. Unless you were here at the time, there is no way to have all the knowledge."

She laughed and asked why I had done the research. I told her that I had written a story about the place from information I had received from Bill Campbell Junior back in the late 50's. She smiled and said she remembered both Bill Senior and Bill Junior. She asked me about the characters. I told her that one was Arizona Charlie. She laughed and said that she knew him. She said that she had met him when she was nineteen years old. I was completely blown away. She said he was a very tall man for that era.

I then told her I had not been able to get any information about the Brothel that used to be upstairs in what was now Palace Hotel. I told her that it was now a lounge called The Jersey Lilly. She laughed and said, "Buy me a beer and I will give you some real history." I was happy to buy her a beer. She told me that she had lived in Prescott all of her life and knew both Arizona Charlie and Wyatt Earp. She said they were both horn dogs.

She mentioned that times were different in those days. Most men did not get married because the West was so wild and they traveled a lot to make a living; whether as a cowboy, a mule-skinner or miner. She also explained that every town had several brothels and the men of the West had their favorite girls so there was really no need to get married.

She went on to say again that it was a tough time with tough ways of living life. There were advantages for both the prostitutes and the patrons. She said that the prostitutes always had business and they did not have to worry about whether their husband was coming home.

Life as a wife was very hard in those days. The married woman had huge responsibilities. Usually the men were gone on cattle drives or mining and the women would run the house and raise the children and, in most cases, also had to have some means of income. Some took in laundry or did some other jobs to make ends meet.

She walked me around the other side of the bar to the dance area and showed me where the dumb waiter was located. A dumb waiter is sort of an elevator with cup like holders. The bartender put the drinks in the dumb waiter and rang the bell and the folks upstairs would pull the chain and bring the drinks upstairs.

She told me the Palace was an upscale bar and that the only places where the prostitutes hung out were in the boomtowns like Tombstone and the mining communities. We finished our beer and she said, "Follow me, Sonny, and you will learn a few things." I was so excited. She went out the front door and turned north toward Gurley and turned into the very first door north of the Palace. It was a door that led to a long stairway.

We went up the stairway and she pointed to a room just at the top of the stairs and told me this was the visiting area. She said the men would mingle with the girls and pick out who they wanted. I asked her how the brothel was tied to the bar. She told me that behind the bar was a show card with a menu of services to be rendered and the price for the services. She said the man would pick out his choice of services and pay the bartender.

According to his desire he was given tokens that indicated his purchase for service and an embroidered special Palace towel. She said the patron would come up the stairs and the madam would take the tokens and then after he chose his lady, the madam would tell the prostitute which services had been established. I asked about the towel. She told me that at the end of the night the girls would turn in their towels and that was how they were paid for their services.

She showed me around the hotel, which is now a bar and offices. In the back of my mind I wanted to ask her how many towels she collected. She just seemed to have a lot more information than most people would think. I did respect her and just kept my thoughts to myself. She was almost proud to show me around. We stepped into the bar and I bought her another beer.

She then told me about another brothel that was located across the street from the now Gurley Street Grill. She said that her nephew came into town sometime in the 30s and inquired about a brothel. She sent him down to this particular establishment and told him to ask for Mary. He said when he arrived and asked for Mary, an older lady told him that Mary was sick and introduced herself as Chris. She said she was Mary's mother and that Mary was sick and she was taking her place so she would not lose her job.

I broke out in a roar. She looked at me and said that it was not funny. She said that jobs were hard to find and everybody had to eat and pay bills. I apologized for being ignorant but I did tell her that it was obvious that times were different in those days.

She told me she remembered when Wyatt Earp and Arizona Charlie passed on in 1929. She said a lot of the old west history died with both of them. I smiled and said that I was totally amazed at her memory and that she was also a big part of the history of the west. She told me she would spend time with me anytime that I wanted to talk about Prescott. I offered to take her home but she said she was in no hurry and that her grandson was coming for her.

I gave her a big hug and left for Phoenix. My mind was going a thousand miles an hour and the ride went by very quickly as I thought about all the history that she had shared with me.

MAYER DAZE

Mayer Daze
By

Zeke Crandall
July 3, 1997

Dedicated To
Thomas G & Thomas A
McCarthy

Chapter One
Hunting - A Guy Thing

It was the first week of October 1956. I was nine years old. We lived in Phoenix, Arizona. Phoenix in 1955 was still considered cowboy country to the folks in the East. Our family was from Nova Scotia and all of my uncles would telephone us to be sure that we were all right. They were under the impression that there were still wild Indians out in Arizona.

The Indians were wild for sure, but not in the wild way my uncles thought. I grew up with several Navajo boys. They were a very proud people but were definitely not wild, a little crazy at times, but who was I to judge. I was definitely a little crazy, so I got along well with them.

Another myth was that they could not hold their liquor. There are people of all nationalities that cannot hold their liquor. The Indians are no different. This was just the white man trying to judge all Indians by a few losers. Heck, I knew a lot of gringos that could not hold their liquor, so that logic did not hold water with me.

Our family was pretty normal. My father worked for Mountain Bell Telephone Company and my mother was a housewife. There was myself, my sister Cathy, and our baby brother George. We were not rich but we were not dirt poor. We lived in a southwest Phoenix, low income neighborhood.

Across the street were our adopted grandparents, Kenny and Mary Harris. These folks were wonderful people. They did not have grandchildren of their own so they treated us like their grandchildren. Kenny in particular definitely spoiled me. He had two great loves other than his wife Mary, playing music and hunting.

Hunting was especially good in the fall and winter months around Mayer, Arizona. Mayer is about seventy-five miles

46

north and west of Phoenix on the way to Prescott. Kenny and his buddy, Rudy Mac, would plan a hunting trip almost every weekend. They were both retired and stayed around the house during the week, but the weekends were reserved for music and hunting.

Being the true gentlemen they always invited their wives, who always promptly declined. Kenny would tell Mary, "Very well, then we will take little Tommy." This was exciting for me because my father did not like to fish or hunt so these two gentlemen helped me respect and love the outdoors. My father was a reader and spent almost all of his leisure time reading.

Kenny signed me up with a gun safety training class that is still held to this day by the Phoenix Jaycees. The Jaycees are a group of Arizona businessmen, mostly born in Arizona. They are dedicated to promoting citizenship for the youngsters in the community.

Kenny was a tremendous shot and a great hunter and he taught me everything there was to know about shooting, tracking and hunting. He had come from Cincinnati but lived most of his life out here in the West. He was a tall fellow, about six feet, thin at about 150 lbs, and partially bald. He always wore a Montana Peak hat.

Friday came and we were on our way out of town right after I arrived home from school. They always reserved a room for us at the two-story hotel, which was the only one in Mayer. It was convenient because the dance hall, bar, grocery store, and the dentist office were right across the street. The dance hall had hardwood floors, which was rare for Arizona. The restaurant was right next to the bar.

We always had dinner at the restaurant and then would head over to the bar or dancehall to set up the instruments. Kenny played the fiddle and Rudy Mac played the banjo. Man, I could not believe it, but they really had a great following. The dance hall would fill up early. Kenny and Rudy Mac had everybody dancing, drinking and generally just having a good time by the second set. I would normally stay for the first two sets. After the second set Kenny usually would come over and say, "Tommy, it's time for you to hit the sack. You have had a long day and we have a big day of hunting planned for tomorrow early in the morning."

Strange thing about the dance hall was that while we were there each night for a short period, I did notice quite a few nice looking women who seemed to be always around Kenny and Rudy Mac. I was only nine, but was starting to see girls in a different way. It never dawned on me that Kenny and Rudy might have a third passion.

On that particular weekend, right after the first set, I noticed a couple come up to the stage and Rudy and Kenny seemed very excited. After shaking hands and hugging each other they headed over to my table, Kenny introduced me to them. He said that they were Hank and Mary Smelser. He told me that they had been life long friends and that Hank would be joining us in the morning to hunt.

Kenny and Rudy had the whole place rocking and in the middle of the second set, I noticed Kenny wave to Hank to join them on the stage. Hank strolled up to the stage. Hank reached into his pocket and pulled out what looked like a harmonica. Then the three of them started playing together and I mean they were really jamming. What a difference an extra instrument can make. It is incredible if it is played with respect to the other musicians and actually adds to the total sound and harmony of the group.

I sat with Mary while they finished the second set. I told her that Hank sounded great and that he was a perfect partner for Kenny and Rudy. She told me that Hank had been playing harmonica from the time he was ten years old. She went on to tell me that Hank had played with Kenny and Rudy on many gigs over the years. She told me that Kenny and Rudy wanted him to join their group but his job as a private investigator just did not permit him to make all of the scheduled gigs.

They would join Kenny and Rudy when scheduling allowed. She said that they truly enjoyed each others company and they really had fun jamming together. Kenny came over and reminded me that it was time to hit the sack. Mrs. Smelser walked me across the street to the hotel and made sure that I was tucked into bed before she said good night and headed back to the dance palace.

About six a.m. I felt someone shaking me. I looked up and it was that Hank Smelser guy. He said, "Tommy, Kenny and Rudy played real late last night and they asked me to take you hunting today." I kind of rubbed the sleep out of my eyes and said "Ok, just let me get ready." He told me to get dressed and meet him at the restaurant across the street from the hotel. I got dressed and headed to the restaurant.

Hank and I finished breakfast and we did not talk much. He mentioned, "Kenny told me that you really enjoyed hunting and that he had taught you how to shoot, track and hunt." I told Hank that I had never known anyone who was a better hunter than Kenny. Hank paid the bill and we headed back across the street to the hotel.

We walked behind the hotel and there was this old black two-door sedan from what looked like the 1930's. Hank said, "Here is my car. Get in and let's go." Well, we got in the old relic, and to my surprise it started right up. Believe it or not the car ran great. We drove about a half hour out of town to an area north and west of Mayer. He stopped the car and said that this looked like a great hunting area. The area was full of young mesquite trees and a lot of grass.

We got out and went around the back of the car. Hank opened the trunk and reached in and pulled out two beautiful

22 caliber rifles. One was a pump model and the other was a lever action model. He told me to pick the one I wanted so I took the pump action model. We loaded the guns and off we went.

We started up the mountain, which was about a mile and a half away. We had hunted about two hours and we both had four rabbits. We came to a rise and I was just getting warmed up. Hank looked at me and said, "Boy I am over seventy and need to rest." We stopped in front of a mineshaft and had an early lunch.

During our lunch break I asked Hank how he knew Kenny and Rudy Mac. He told me that they had met many years ago in Flagstaff. He said that they became friends when he asked them if he could join them to play a few tunes. He said that they instantly jammed and felt very comfortable playing with each other. He said that they sounded like they had played together for years.

From that day forward, if Hank was in the crowd, Kenny and Rudy would call him up to the stage to join them for a couple of sets. He said that it was impossible for him to play with them on a permanent basis because his job did not permit him to always make the gigs.

He pulled a harmonica out of his pocket and said, "Little Tommy, have you blown into a harmonica?" I told him no. He played for about ten minutes and he definitely was great. He told me that the harmonica was a perfect instrument and he went on to say that it could be used for rhythm or lead. He handed me another harmonica that he had in his other pocket and began to give me lessons.

To my surprise I picked it up right away. He explained that the draw notes were the filler notes and that it was important to learn to blow and draw. Our early lunch ended up being a three hour music lesson. The harmonica aroused an interest in me that had never known before. That three hours seemed to fly by.

We set out walking back to the car, which we could see was about two miles away. We were able to get a few more shots off and Hank was definitely a good shot. He picked up two more rabbits on the way back and I was able to get one more. We gutted, cleaned and skinned the rabbits and Hank put them in plastic bags for safe- keeping.

While we cleaned and gutted the rabbits, Hank told me that a hunter never takes anything unless he is going to eat that animal. He said that real hunters do not kill just to kill. He put the rabbits in a cooler that he had in the trunk. We washed our hands by holding the five gallon containers and pouring the water over our hands.

We dried our hands and just before he shut the trunk he said, "Wait a minute, I have something for you." He reached in this pouch and pulled out a shiny new harmonica and handed it to me and said, "Tommy, here, this is for you. I think it will bring you a lot of pleasure." He told me that practice makes perfect and that I needed to practice a lot if I expected to be proficient with any instrument. When we got back to the hotel he let me off in front of the hotel and I said thank you. That was the last time that I saw Hank Smelser.

Kenny and Rudy were already packed and ready to go. I went across the street to the dance hall and met them and we all got into the car and headed for home. When we got in the car I told Kenny and Rudy about my day of hunting with Hank. I showed them the harmonica that he gave me. Kenny told me that Hank was a very colorful guy.

Kenny went on to say that Hank had been a private investigator of some renown in Arizona many years ago before retiring. They told me that he had been a good friend of Tom Mix, the famous western cowboy actor. They said that Tom spent a lot of time here in Arizona and had his own studio outside of Prescott.

A funny thing happened as we were driving out of town. We drove about a half mile and there was this beautiful white two story house that I could see out of my window on the passenger side of the car. It was a large house with a porch in front that extended along one side of the building. There was a porch on the main floor and one on the second floor. I noticed as we were driving by that there were about eight women out front waving goodbye to both Kenny and Rudy.

I was just a little boy but I thought this was a little strange so I asked Grandpa Kenny, "What is that place? Who are those ladies that are waving our way?" Rudy Mac said, "That place is a bordello and those ladies are..." Kenny jumped in and stopped Rudy from going on and said, "It is a boarding house for women, and they work at the hotel and the dance hall."

I said to them, "Look at that red-headed lady on the upper balcony waving to you guys. It looks like she is wearing her underwear!" Kenny jumped in and said, "Tommy, those are bloomers." I had no idea what bloomers were but I dropped the subject and fell asleep on the ride back.

The next day on my walk to school I kept thinking about the ladies. I was getting to the age where I was attracted to women. I was thinking about that good- looking redhead on the second story balcony and I thought that I once saw my mother in those so called bloomers one morning early working around the house. I was just as sure that the redhead was in her underwear.

Anyway, after contemplating the house and the ladies I decided to put it to rest. One thing for sure, Grandma Mary would surely not understand those ladies. Several years later, one of my worldly friends told me the definition of a bordello. I knew then that it was a good thing that I did not say anything to Grandma Mary.

What a trip these guys were. All that time I thought we were there to hunt rabbits, but at night after I was asleep, Kenny and Rudy were hunting beaver, I mean two-legged beaver. One thing was for sure. They were bagging way more than their limit. I kept the incident to myself and never said anything to Grandma Mary. What a couple of rascals. My only regret was that I was not a couple of years older so that I could have gone to the "Boarding House." I could have checked out the redhead in the bloomers myself.

Chapter Two
The Fog

The alarm radio went off as usual, waking up to the Beth and Bill show in the morning. But this was Saturday and neither Rose, my wife, or I had to go to work. We looked forward to a great weekend that we had planned. It was Saturday Oct 3, 1995. It was Parent's Weekend at Northern Arizona University in Flagstaff. We had reservations at the Little America Hotel. We were looking forward to spending a weekend with our sons Tom and Dan who were students at the college.

I headed for the kitchen to make a pot of coffee while Rose showered and got dressed. After she finished, I took a shower and got dressed. I loaded our bags in our new 1995 Ford Explorer. I had just come back in the house and I heard her call to me, "Make sure you bring your harmonicas." I said, "Of course, you just never know." We headed to the kitchen and finished our coffee.

We were looking forward to the trip. According to the paper it looked like we would run into some bad weather on the way. We finished the cup of coffee and poured another cup for the road. We stopped at the Mobil Station and filled up the car and then headed to Interstate 17.

I turned on the radio to catch the current weather report. We were listening to our favorite station 99.9 and then Marty Manning broke in to update us on the current weather conditions. Rose and I both chuckled because Marty was one of my Phoenix College fraternity brothers and we always enjoyed listening to him. Well anyway, he predicted that we would run into rain.

Rose looked a little worried, so I explained we would be okay because this was a four wheel drive vehicle. I told her that we would be plenty safe. I guess Rose must have been pretty tired. She told me that she had a tough week. She fell asleep about fifty miles north of Phoenix. About fifteen miles further, we came to the turnoff to Prescott which was State Route 69.

I looked over at Rose while she slept and had a smile on my face as I recalled my boyhood hunting trips with Kenny and Rudy Mac. I realized that Mayer was only about ten miles west from us on State Route 69. I wondered if the hotel was still there along with the big white two-story home with those scantily dressed women. I just burst out laughing when I thought about Kenny changing Rudy's pronouncement of bordello to a boarding house for women.

When I burst out laughing, I woke up Rose. She looked at me and said, "Tom, what are you laughing about?" I said, "Nothing really. Bill told a joke that I thought was really funny." She said, "But the radio is off." I replied, "I know, he told the joke about 20 minutes ago and it just dawned on me, that it was a great punch line." She looked at me strangely. I thought to myself, "A small white lie is better than the truth in this situation."

We were just passing the Oak Creek turnoff going north on I-17 and heading up the hill to the Mogollon Rim. The Rim runs from just west of the interstate all the way east to Payson. It rises some 2,000 feet from 5,000 feet to 7,200 feet. Flagstaff is about forty-five miles from where the rim begins. We were about eight miles south of the Stoneman Lake Road exit.

We had both noticed it was cloudy ahead as we started up the hill past the Oak Creek exit. This was pretty normal for the area. There was usually cloud cover just as you got to the rim. But, this day was a little different. We encountered ominous fog. It looked like there was a lot of moisture in the fog along with some type of lightning.

Rose was a little frightened, and I might add that I was also a little scared. I heeded her suggestion and pulled over to the side of the road after driving about a mile or so. The fog was so thick that we could not see but about five feet in front of us even with our bright lights. We stayed on the side of the road for about a half hour or so until it cleared enough to proceed.

Starting out again and barely out of the fog, I noticed a vehicle coming toward us in the left lane. It happened so quickly that it scared me. I was concerned that the driver had made a mistake and got on the wrong side of the freeway so I pulled over again onto the right shoulder of the road. As the car went by us I took a second look at the car and the driver. I stared at the car in amazement.

The driver just smiled at us and waved as he went by. The vehicle was a vintage 1930's black two-door sedan with a rumble seat. I exclaimed out loud as the car was passing, "Rose, did you see that idiot waving to us like there was nothing wrong? Did you see the car he was driving? It looks like it is brand new!" She quickly replied, "Who in the world is Rose?" I looked over my right shoulder and there was a woman sitting next to me that I had never laid eyes on ever in my entire life.

I said to her, "Who in the world are you?" She looked at me with amazement. She then said, "I am your wife, Mary, but who is Rose? Is she a girlfriend of yours or just someone you met in a bar while playing music with your buddies?" I said to her, "Rose is my wife." She said, "Are you crazy, I'm Mary, and I'm your wife." She went on to say, "Is there something wrong with you?"

She continued, "Hank, we need to get to Flagstaff as soon as possible. Clyde and the gang are waiting for us and you know they will be getting impatient. My sister wants us at their home for lunch." Then I asked, "Who the hell is Hank?" She said, "You are Hank Smelser and I am Mary Smelser, your wife." I replied, "Boy, I must really be crazy, because my name is Tom."

She then said, "Well, your name has been Hank for as long as I can remember." I was really shook up now. I thought for a minute and then realized that I remembered that name. It was definitely way in the past, but what was I doing here and what in the world was happening. I did not know what to say. I happened to glance up in the rearview mirror to see if it was clear to proceed, and there to my surprise, was the face of a man that I had never seen in my life. I knew one thing for sure, it was not Tom.

I did not recognize the person. It was a gentleman about 35 years old, handlebar moustache, curly blonde hair and a little heavy set. I was so shocked and confused that I got out of the car. I walked around to the front of the car and there to my disbelief the vehicle I was driving was a 1930's black model four door Ford Sedan.

This lady, Mary, got out of the car and started walking toward me. This was my first look at her outside of the car. She was about 5'8", weighed about 115 lbs. She had long black hair with dark hazel eyes. She was a fairly attractive woman, and appeared well dressed, and carried herself with dignity. I could see she was definitely upset.

She ran up and gave me a bear hug and a kiss. She said, "What is wrong with you Hank, you look like you just saw a ghost." She held my hand and led me back to the car. She said, "Please, could we go on to Flagstaff, and when you see the boys everything will be all right."

The road was in good shape. It was a paved two lane road the rest of the way to Flagstaff. I was not used to driving this old vehicle and on these old roads. I tried to get the darn thing to build a little speed but no matter how hard I pushed on the gas pedal, the vehicle would not go over forty m.p.h. I was definitely a very confused person to say the least. I kept wondering about who exactly was this gang that Mary was talking about.

Chapter Three
Flagstaff & the Case

We arrived about an hour later. It seemed like that fifty miles took forever. We went by Old Main to our right, on the Northern Arizona College campus. We proceeded north and went under the railroad tunnel, then turned right and were now on Santa Fe Street. We stopped about a half-mile later at the Beaver Street exit. We stopped at a bar on the northeast corner of Beaver and Santa Fe. I was given all of these directions with the help of Mary, who was supposed to be my wife.

We parked the car out front and went into the saloon. The bar was simply called Beaver Street. I held Mary's hand, and just as we entered the bar, we went to the right to a table up against a window facing Santa Fe Street. She could tell that I was still definitely shook up. All I could think about was Rose. Where was she?

There were several people sitting at the table. One of them yelled, "How come it took you folks so long to get here?" Mary replies, "Ask Hank, but before you do, ask him to order us a drink because it might take a while to explain our adventure and I am thirsty." The bartender said, "The usual?" Mary replied, "Sure."

Then the bartender brought each of us a rum and coke. I said to the bartender, "Don't take anything personal, but can I have a cold mug of draft beer?" Mary then said, "Hank, what are you doing drinking beer? In all of the years I have known you, you have never had a beer." I downed the beer in about ten minutes and ordered another mug. On the next mug, I swirled the beer around in my mouth. It tasted wonderful.

Then the guy sitting next to me asked me why it took so long for us to arrive. He asked me if everything was all right.

I said, "No, but it really doesn't matter." He said, "Hank, it does matter to me, hell we have been good friends for over twenty years." I took another gulp of beer and asked him, "Who are you and how long have I known you?" He looked astonished and said, "I'm Clyde. We have been friends since our college days. We both were in the graduating class at Northern Arizona State College."

Another guy was standing next to Clyde. Clyde looked at me and said, "You remember Mark. We have been friends since our freshman year in college. We all worked on the project together our senior year in college as part of our astronomy class." I said, "What project do you mean?" Clyde went on to say, "Our friend Percy Lowell started the discovery of Pluto. You and Mark worked with me to finish the project and I actually discovered the planet the next weekend that you were both out of town."

"Ah yes, you are Clyde Tombaugh," I said. "I know you from reading about your scientific discovery that took place right here at the college observatory." Clyde looked stunned and said, "Reading about the discovery? Don't you remember our experiences while working on the project together?" He dropped the discussion with a look of disbelief. He turned to Mary and said, "I think Hank has amnesia."

Clyde goes on to say, "Mark here has become one of the best chemists of our time. He specializes in collecting physical evidence from crime scenes. He is on the cutting edge of crime investigation. Hank, in your line of work, Mark has become an invaluable asset." I said, "What is my business?" Clyde said, "You goofball, you are a private investigator. I know that I have not been much help to you as an astronomer."

Clyde motioned to Mark to come over and join them at their table. Clyde mentioned, "You know, Mark has been a great asset in your line of business." You both have become one of the best investigative teams in the country. Mark has been getting calls from police departments from all across the country. Mark has begun to travel the country cracking tough cases for local police departments. He gets a flat fee and all of his expenses are paid. He still enjoys working with you since you helped give him the start in his career. I have remained close to both of you over the years because we have had so many great experiences together since our college days."

I finished the mug of beer and ordered another. Mary commented, "Hank, I have never seen you drink anything that quickly, let alone it be a mug of beer." I thought to myself, "Yes, because I am not Hank, my name is Tom, and I love beer." I can take a rum and coke, but if I had my druthers it would be a cold mug of draft beer. Boy, I will tell you, that beer tasted so good. Maybe it was because it was the only real thing in my life, for right now anyway.

Mary looked at me and said, "Hank, we need to slow down, we still have to go to lunch at my sister, Ann's house. You know her husband, Steve, is waiting to talk with you about the recent murder of Flagstaff librarian, Miss Amy Wilson." I looked at her and she said, "Ann is my sister and her husband is my brother-in-law Steve, who happens to be the Chief of Police here in Flagstaff. The murder is the reason we are up here this weekend. Steve needs your expertise in helping to solve the murder of Miss Wilson."

By this time my head was spinning with all of this crazy investigation talk. I thought to myself, "Heck, I'm just a computer salesman." I had once worked as an adjuster for a couple of insurance companies and was definitely well trained in claim handling and investigation. A private eye though? Are you kidding me? No way can I pull this one off I thought. They will surely figure me out. Heck, these people are killing me.

A few minutes later, this big guy walks over toward me from the other side of the bar and slapped me on the back and said, "Hank, how the hell are you." I looked up and thought I recognized this guy. I had really been into the original cowboy actors and this guy looked like Tom Mix. He wore a big white cowboy hat and was wearing a beautiful white leather jacket. I said to him, "Is that you Tom?" He laughed and said, "Of course it is me." Mary looked at me and interrupted us by saying, "Well Tom, it looks like you have helped Hank with his amnesia."

Really, I did not know any of these people but I did recognize Tom from my reading. He went on to say, "What is with that beer in your hand?" I have known you for so many years with the two of us sharing so many good times and you always drinking rum and coke. I have never seen you drink beer. This is a great experience being able to share a cold one with you after all of these years. It seems like you are really enjoying that mug of beer." I told him that I was definitely enjoying the cold draft beer.

Tom lifted the mug and asked me if he could offer a toast. I told him, "Go right ahead, big guy." He laughed and said to me, "You have always called me big guy." He said that he really got a kick out of it. I laughed too, but for a different reason. I thought it was an obvious remark but I had no idea that it was the same nickname that this guy Hank called him, definitely a strange and lucky similarity.

Tom went on to say, "Here, I would like to toast one of the best investigators of all time." The whole gang including Mary joined the toast. I really felt special. All of these great people of the past toasting me and not roasting me. Tom went on with the toast by saying, "I should know a great investigator since I have known all of the great lawmen of the old west. You are the best I have ever met."

Tom went on to thank me for the great work that I did in tracking down a psycho fan that had threatened him and his family. I thanked him for the compliment but went on to tell him that I could not have completed the investigation without the help of Mark. I also thanked him for paying me so well for the job. Tom went on to say that I just charged him the going rate but it was a minor price to pay for finding the culprit and giving back a life to him and his family.

As I drank the rest of the mug of beer many thoughts popped into my head. How did I know these facts about this case, this was long before I was even born. Maybe I really was this guy Hank Smelser. I was very confused and felt very strange. I did feel comfortable right then in the bar. It was like I had been there before. Tom gave Mary a big hug and shook hands with Mark and Clyde. He turned to me and invited me outside to see his new car.

As we went through the swinging, old time saloon doors, I looked over my right shoulder and I just knew which car was his. I had seen it when we pulled in the parking lot but I was so shook up that I did not give it much thought. He went right up the car and pointed to it and asked me what I thought. There was this beautiful 1934 Chorde two door, two-seater white sports car, with a hood ornament made of longhorn steer horns. The interior was all cowhide leather.

It was definitely a beautiful car and I had seen pictures of it on the Internet when I was researching Tom Mix. He had the car built to his specifications. But now I was looking at the real thing. It was a great experience. Tom threw me the keys and said, "Let's jump in and take it for a spin." I was thrilled to say the least. I jumped in and got behind the steering wheel like a little kid and Tom sat in the passenger seat. I backed the car out onto Beaver Street and headed northbound.

This car was really special. It had a steering wheel that was made of cowhide and the dash was made of leather also. We went out of town toward Humphrey's Peak, and Tom told me to punch it and see how well the car handled. I did exactly as he told me and the car really did handle well. I had the car up to eighty miles per hour. That was amazing for 1934. We turned around and headed back to the saloon.

Tom spoke as we were riding back, "Hank, I was proud to let you drive the car and you have not missed a beat. You are still one of the best drivers that I have ever ridden with. You should have been a race car driver." I did not think about what he said until we got back to the saloon. I thanked him for letting me drive his new car and I told him that it handled great and that I loved the car and that I was in awe of its sheer beauty. I told him that it was definitely a real runner.

We arrived back at the bar and got out of the car and were heading back into the saloon. Mary was coming out and met us just outside the doors. She said to me, "Hank, we need to be going because my sister and Steve are waiting for us before they begin lunch. Ann just called to see why we were running late. I told her we would be right over. I told her that you were out for a spin in Tom's new car with him and she laughed. Tom, my sister told me that you were in town visiting, and that you had been working on a movie at your studio at Yavapai Hills."

Tom said "Yes, but I knew that Hank was coming and I would not miss seeing you folks for the world." I asked Mary if I could go back into the bar to say goodbye to my new friends. She said, "Go right ahead if you think you need to say goodbye, but they are expecting to see us tonight at Mormon Lake Lodge for dinner and an evening of dancing."

Tom said to us, "Your old musician friends will be playing at the Lodge tonight and they are looking forward to playing some tunes with their old harmonica playing buddy

Hank. It is always a blast when you jam and we are all together."

I thought to myself, "At least I have one thing in common with this Hank guy since I play the harmonica." That is when it hit me that this guy Hank had been the person that introduced me to the harmonica when I was about nine years old. I definitely felt a little strange. This body I had did not look like the Hank that I met when I was a child. He was an old man when I met him. I did see a resemblance in Mary though. I had met him and her only one time in my life and that was a long time ago.

We got in the car and headed over to Steve and Ann's for lunch. I was excited about discussing the murder case with him. On our way over to their house, Mary said that her sister's dressmaking shop was exploding. She said her sister had a great idea. She wanted to expand and open a shop in Phoenix. I then guessed that Mary was also a seamstress.

We headed west on Santa Fe toward the observatory past the turnoff to Milton, which is where the road turned south and went under the railroad tracks. This was the way that we came into town. We just passed the turn and it was then I noticed this beautiful two-story large brick home on the north side of Santa Fe. The house was about a half mile down the road. I was about to comment on the beautiful home when Mary yelled, "Hank stop, where are you going, you are about to pass the house!"

I must have been daydreaming about the observatory. That is the first thought that passed through my mind. I pulled right in driveway of the large two-story block home as if I had been there many times. I had hoped that this was the right home. Sure enough we stopped and Mary got out and seemed all excited. This lady came out of the front door and I could have sworn that I thought I was seeing Mary. Ann and

Mary were twins. They hugged each other and Ann hugged me.

As we approached the door, I could smell the fresh cornbread. We entered the home and hung our jackets up in the entry way on a coat rack. I looked over my right shoulder and into the living room, and this guy was sitting in a rocking chair reading the morning paper. He put it down and said, "Good afternoon Hank." He stood up and kept standing. This guy was probably 6'4 or 6'5 and weighed well over two hundred pounds. He had a large handlebar mustache. He shook my hand and said he was glad that we came up.

I still could not get over the resemblance of the two ladies. Ann spoke up, "Hank, I made your favorite, ham and beans with fresh cornbread." I didn't know if it was my favorite, but it smelled great and I was really hungry. Steve remarked, "We're starving and Ann made me wait until you folks arrived for lunch. And none to soon." he added. He asked if we enjoyed the visit with his friends.

Steve said, "Tom came by earlier to see you folks, but I told him that you guys would probably head to the saloon. He told us he was taking a break from doing a movie at his studio near Prescott. He told us that your musician buddies called him to tell him that you and Mary were coming up for the weekend." Steve went on, "Tom headed to the saloon and said that they all planned to meet at Mormon Lake Lodge for dinner and a great evening and he invited me and Ann."

I told Steve that I had seen them all and really enjoyed a couple of drinks with them. I began to feel a little more comfortable within my surroundings. I still could not figure out why I was there and what happened to Tom and Rose. We all went to the dining room and as the girls began to set the table we went on into the kitchen. Steve went over to the icebox and told me that he would be happy to make me a rum and coke.

When Steve opened the icebox door I noticed a few bottles of beer. He reached in for a bottle and I asked him if I could join him with a bottle of beer rather than the mixed drink. He smiled and said, "I don't believe it, you want a beer?" I said "Yes, is there something wrong with beer?" He said no, but that he had never seen me drink a beer, ever. I told him that I had acquired a taste for beer and could not believe what I had been missing. Boy was that a crock of bullshit, but it sounded good so what the hell.

Steve told me that Kenny and Rudy had called him earlier to make sure that their music-playing buddy had arrived safely. He told me that we needed to call them at the hotel to let them know that we had arrived safely. He called the Hotel Weatherford and asked for Kenny's room. The deskman tried to connect us but there was nobody in the room. He left a message for Kenny and Rudy indicating that Hank and Mary had arrived safely. After he hung up the phone he turned to me and said, "They are probably over at the saloon with Tom and the gang." We will surely see them all later.

Just then Ann said, "Come on everybody, lunch is ready." I told Steve that I needed to wash up for lunch and that they could go ahead and start without me. They all said great. They sat down and started to have lunch and I headed for the restroom. I entered the bathroom and turned on the light then turned on the faucets to fill the basin. I was afraid to look in the mirror but I had no choice. As I looked, I was completely amazed again at what I was seeing in the mirror. I washed up and headed to the dining room with a lot of weird thoughts entering my head.

Steve looked and me and said, "Hank, you look a little green around the gills." You look like you just saw a ghost. I laughed, I don't know about ghosts but I still could not figure out what was going on." I told Steve that everything was all right but that I was simply starving. I sat down and joined them. I complimented Ann on such a wonderful lunch.

Steve told me that he helped make the cornbread. We all laughed and I commented that they made a good team. We finished lunch and I commended Ann and Steve on a fine job preparing such a fine feast. Ann poured us a cup of coffee and Steve and I went into the den. He sat on the rocking chair and I sat on the sofa that was located under the front room window. The ladies went upstairs to Ann's sewing room and combination home office for her seamstress shop.

Steve lit his pipe with a special cherry blend tobacco. The scent had a very calming effect but I had no desire to take up smoking just so I could enjoy the smell. I could see the bowl get red in color because the bowl was very hot. This indicated that the pipe had been broken in.

He then started talking about the Amy Wilson murder case. He went over a brief summary of the facts surrounding her death. I said, "Well Steve, I guess we might as well head over to your office so I can see all of the evidence, and we can go over all of the facts and the crime team photos. Steve said to me, "Hank, we will stop by the scene of the crime. It happens to be right on the way to my office."

We drove again east on Santa Fe and turned north on Aspen Street which was one block east of Beaver Street. As we were turning, I looked down at my watch and noticed it was 2:30 p.m. I could see that Tom's car was still parked in front of the saloon. I think we went about one block north on Aspen and I noticed this beautiful big two-story hotel on the side of the street just south of the intersection of Aspen and Leroux, which was the first street running east and west one block north of Santa Fe.

We stopped and parked in front of the hotel and got out and entered the hotel from the Aspen street entrance. We went by the front desk and the attendant waved to Steve. I am sure that after all of the investigation that they knew each other well. We proceeded up the stairs to the third floor. At the top of the stairway to the left was the Zane Grey Room, which was the lounge for the hotel.

As we climbed the stairs I noticed that the hotel rooms were on the 2nd floor and also when we reached the third floor there were more hotel rooms to the right at the top of the stairs. We entered the lounge right at the top of the stairs. We went by the bar, which was to our left.

We turned left and headed toward the Leroux Street exit. We went through the side exit to the porch just outside the lounge. Steve walked up to the rail directly in line from the two-door swinging exit. He asked me to look over the rail at the cement sidewalk some twenty feet below. I told him that it was sure a long way down. He then showed me some scratches on the floor.

Steve went on to say that Amy was a local school teacher, but that she worked at the Zane Grey Lounge on the weekends to make ends meet. He said that it looked like she had been pushed over the rail, which by the way, was about three feet high and ran about ten feet between the posts. He said by the look of trauma on her head that she died instantly when she hit the pavement. He told me that their investigation indicated that she had no enemies. He asked me if I wanted to look around and I told him no, that I wanted to go to his office and look at the file.

The police station was only one block north of us so we walked over. Steve went right to his office and handed me the file from his desk. I started going over the evidence in the file. The lounge closed at 1 a.m., and the time of death about 2 a.m.

I asked Steve if anybody saw anyone talking with her before the end of her shift. Steve went on to say, "No, we have already checked with all of those folks. There was nobody there at the time of the murder other than one of the local patrons. He left just before the murder. We checked out his alibi and it was up to snuff."

I then started viewing the pictures of the body. She was a beautiful lady of slight build, probably no more than 105 lbs, and tall at about 5'7" with light brown hair and blue eyes. It looked like she was trying to tell me something. If you look closely they actually can tell you a story. I did note in one of the pictures that she had a large bruise on her left wrist. It looked like someone had held her by the wrist very tightly. We could see a very large bruise that was completely surrounding her wrist.

In another picture I noticed that she had bruises on the right side of her throat and only one on the left side of her throat. I told Steve that we were looking for a left-handed suspect. I told him that the evidence indicated that the perpetrator grabbed her left hand with his right hand and then had his dominant left hand around her throat. I went on to say that this should help narrow the suspects. He looked at me and said, "Well Hank, this is the reason you are here." I asked him if we could take the file so I could study it a little further. He said, "Fine."

I then asked him if we could stop back at the scene on the way back to the car so I could have another look at the physical evidence. As we entered the lounge again, I pointed to the floor at some other scratches on the floor. I told him that the evidence indicated that she and the perpetrator had probably quarreled and he was holding her by the hand very tightly, indicating he was enraged.

The bruises around her throat indicated that she was not held nearly as tight around the neck. It looked like he swung her around somehow and when he let her go she flew out the double doors and when she hit the rail the force of the push or throw continued and she went right over the rail. I told him that it was a crime of passion and I did not believe that it was a premeditated murder.

The perpetrator was probably too scared to stick around or, maybe had other scrapes with the law or simply felt he would not be treated fairly. I told him that nobody saw anyone leave or enter the lounge before closing time. We were probably looking for a guest of the hotel and he or she is left-handed and probably has a temper.

I asked him if we could stop by the front desk on the way out so we could look at the hotel register for the day of the murder. We stopped at the bar on the way out and I asked the bartender, Bob, if he remembered if any left- handed customers were in the bar the evening of the crime. He looked at me and said, "There was a left- handed customer in the bar that evening earlier, and the customer did spend a lot of time talking with Amy."

Bob went on to say that the customer's name was Shorty McDonald. He was a ranch hand at the Fox cattle ranch about ten miles south of Flagstaff. He continued to say, "Shorty and a couple of other ranch hands came to town to party every other weekend and many times Shorty would just crash at the hotel after a long night of partying rather than try to ride back to the ranch."

Bob went on to say that Shorty had been known to run with the Cowboy gang out of Tombstone before he moved to the Flagstaff area. We said thanks to Bob for being so helpful. We then went down to the front desk to examine the guest log. Sure enough, Shorty was a guest on Saturday, the evening of the crime, and the Friday evening before.

Steve looked at me and said, "Hank, it is just hard to believe that someone could be stupid enough to kill a person and then spend the night in the same hotel." I told Steve, "It would make sense if the perpetrator was grief stricken. He or she may not have meant to kill Amy." I told Steve, "I know stranger things have occurred but if you just look at all of the facts and evidence it is obvious.   I know exactly what happened."

I explained, "This Shorty guy probably loved Amy and was very distraught.   He was probably afraid to say anything because he ran with such a notorious gang like the Cowboys. He thought he would be found guilty, and not be given a fair trial.   No Steve, we are not looking for a dangerous criminal and if we confront him I believe he will breakdown."

Steve looked at me and said, "Hank," lets go get ready for tonight."   The girls are probably waiting for us.   It is now 4:30 pm and we have been at this for over two hours."   He smiled at me and I said, "Yeah, two hours but it appears the case is solved."   Steve told me that he would get the warrant for the arrest of Shorty on Sunday.   He said he knew the judge and there would be no problem getting a warrant once he went over the facts.

Steve went on to say that we needed to get home and freshen up.   We were supposed to meet the gang at Mormon Lake Lodge at 6 p.m. and it was a forty-five minute drive from Flagstaff to the lodge.   We hurried on home and as we entered the front door, Mary turned around toward the kitchen and told Ann, "There, remember how I told you that Hank just gets engrossed in these types of cases."   Steve said, "Yes he does get engrossed and thank God for his ability because he basically solved the case.   We think we know the suspect and how it happened.   Someday we will share the evidence as uncovered by my illustrious brother-in-law, Hank."

Kenny Harris playing guitar and Rudy Mac playing banjo.

Chapter Four
Mormon Lake Lodge

The girls both got on us about getting ready for dinner as soon as possible, because it was now almost 5:00 and we needed to be out of town and on the road to Mormon Lake by 5:15 at the latest. I hurried up the stairs and entered the bathroom next to our bedroom. Steve headed for the master bath, which was downstairs on the other side of the living room. As I walked thru our room, I noticed that Mary unpacked our bags and hung the clothes in the closet.

I pulled my new blue seersucker, three-piece suit, with a white shirt and my dress black wingtip shoes. I then headed to the bathroom to change. As I was washing up for dinner, I noticed the guy looking back at me in the mirror. This time I was not as shook up.

I was starting to get comfortable with this guy in the mirror. Somehow I was pulling out the right answers. I had a little investigative experience but I had no clue how this new found investigative knowledge had been bestowed upon me. I had been trained as an insurance adjuster but this was a whole new ball game. How I figured out that crazy crime earlier that day still dumbfounded me. I was now starting to wonder if I was actually Hank and this guy Tom was a dream.

All I wanted now was to have dinner and get ready for any more crazy situations. I probably fit right in again out of pure luck. I always wanted to have a body like this guy Hank so it was kind of fun. One thing for sure is that at least this guy did not have asthma and I did not have to worry about allergic reactions.

I guess my main thought was how I would act with Mary. I had really not spent a lot of time alone with her. She would surely see through me, and know that I was thinking about my real wife, Rose. Heck, I had plenty of peyote trips in the

1960's, so I figured I would just go with it because I really did not have many choices.

Steve decided to drive so we piled in his four door black Ford sedan and headed to Mormon Lake. We drove about two miles south of Flagstaff and we headed east on the Mormon Lake Road, which was a two-lane dirt and cinder road. There was not very much dust. Steve said that there was a mountain just east of Flagstaff that was made of black volcanic soft rock so plentiful that the cinders were used instead of dirt. He said it kept the dust down.

It took us about forty minutes to arrive as it was about a twenty-five mile drive from the main exit. We arrived at one minute to six. We parked out front on a cinder parking lot. I really liked the cinder roads and lots. The tires gripped the road and the thin tires hardly threw up any rocks. There was relatively no dust. This fact alone is remarkable for the desert in Arizona.

When we entered the restaurant, straight ahead was the lounge. There was a room to the right which was a dining area and a much larger room to the left also for dining. The stage was against the back wall of the main entrance just behind the bar. It was a large elongated wrap around bar that extended about forty feet. I could see two guys setting up instruments on the stage.

Tom, Clyde, Mark and their women were sitting to the left of the stage along the wall that separated the lounge from the left dining area. Tom waved us to come join them. Tom had already ordered a drink for us and they were sitting on the table. Tom smiled and said, "Look Hank, I even remembered to get you a cold mug of beer." I said, "Tom, how long have the drinks been sitting on the table, because they still feel cold."

Clyde laughed and said, "Hank, we can always count on you to be exactly on time. You are like a watch. We knew when you walked in that it would be 6 p.m. so we just planned on you being here." I laughed and thought to myself, "Well, we had another thing in common." I believe that there is no excuse for being late. It is all a matter of planning.

The waiter came over to take our dinner order. He said that everybody else had already placed their orders and he was just waiting for us. I looked at Clyde and said, "What do you suggest?" He said, "Always go with the house special. In this case, it is the mesquite barbequed porterhouse steak, either 12 or 16 ounces, along with a baked potato, cowboy beans and fresh country bread. I looked at Clyde and Mary and said, "Sounds great to me. Mary ordered the 12 oz steak and I ordered the 16 oz.

Tom seized the moment and ordered another round of drinks for all of us. I got up to go to the bathroom to wash my hands before dinner. As I was drying them with a towel, I noticed a copy of the front page of the daily paper hanging on the wall. The date was September 1, 1932. That paper put me in a bummer mood again. I walked out of the restroom and walked by Tom, Clyde, Mark and Steve and did not say anything.

I sat down at the table and had a sip of beer. Tom looked over and said, "Hank, you look like you just saw a ghost." He went on to say, "You look a little green, do you have stomach problems?" Mary told them I had been acting a little peculiar all day. I figured that she knew something was not right but she kept it to herself. I knew that when we were alone that she would probably confront me. But, I figured I would not rush the situation. What would be would be.

I said to them, "Well, in a way I have seen a ghost." They all laughed and Mark said, I think that the beer is taking a toll on your brain." I guzzled the rest of the mug of beer and ordered another. Just after we finished dinner, I noticed two women sitting across the dance floor at a table in between the bar and the stage. I asked Ann if she knew the ladies.

Ann said that one of the ladies was an artist from Cincinnati, Ohio. Ann told us that her name was Blanche Wait, and the other lady was her sister Mary. "They are here for the annual Flagstaff Art Festival. Blanche is a well-known artist in the Cincinnati area and is president of the Art Guild. She is introducing her charcoal collection. She had her oil paintings on display last year. Her sister is a school teacher and traveling companion."

Just as Ann finished speaking about the ladies, I felt a slap on the back and when I turned I noticed that it was Kenny Harris and Rudy Mac. I could not help but stare at them in amazement. Before I was this guy Hank, when I was little Tommy, these two men were my main influence and took me hunting and to their music gigs all around the northern part of the state of Arizona.

Seeing them so young was very energizing. They looked like they were in their middle thirties and looked a whole lot different than when I knew them. They both looked vibrant and full of life. When I met them later in life they were old and tired from the toils of life.

Then, I just knew that I had to meet the ladies. Kenny beat me to the punch. He invited the ladies over to join us at our table. I knew that according to the date on the wall in the bathroom that Blanche would be dead in two years from a form of cancer. I knew that I would really enjoy meeting her. I had studied her work and actually owned a lot of it, so it was very enjoyable meeting her. I also enjoyed meeting Mary, who was her older sister. We chatted for a few minutes.

Kenny then asked me if I brought my harps. Mary, my supposed wife, piped up and said, "Yes Kenny, I made sure that Hank brought his harps." Kenny smiled and said that it just would not be a complete evening if I did not jam with them for a couple of sets. I looked at both Kenny and Rudy and said, "I would not miss jamming with you guys for all of the tea in China."

Kenny then said, "Hank, I just noticed that you were drinking a draft beer. When did you start drinking beer. In all of the years that I have known you, you drank rum and coke." By now, I was getting pretty tired of this statement. I told them all that I enjoyed beer and that I did not want to hear about it again. I thought I would pull a prank on them so I looked at Kenny and said, "Hell, I wasn't old enough to drink when I first met you and Rudy." I quickly turned away and left him pondering that statement.

This was the same Kenny Harris that lived across the street from my family on West Taylor Street, when we first moved to Phoenix. Mary Wait was his wife. We adopted them as our Arizona Grandparents since we had no family here in Arizona and neither did they.

I wanted to ask about Mary, but it was obvious that something was not right. Kenny must have read my mind. He said that he and Rudy had just met the Wait sisters the night before and they had struck up a conversation. Kenny said that they had mutual friends because ironically he was originally from Cincinnati himself. I was just astounded at how good Kenny and Rudy looked. I really looked forward to jamming with them. I knew for sure that Kenny could play the heck out of the fiddle and Rudy was a master with the banjo and they both could sing.

It has always amazed me how musicians are able to play an instrument and sing. It really takes a lot of talent. I never dreamed that I would have this opportunity to play with them. By the time I got proficient with the harmonica in real life, all of these characters were long dead.

Kenny said that they had to start the first set, and that he would wave at me when it was time to join them. I said,

"Great." I ordered another mug of cold beer and then we all proceeded to enjoy the music. Those two really sounded great. It was obvious that they had played a lot together because their music was really tight.

The whole place was really rocking and there were a lot of folks up dancing just before the end of that first set. By this time I was starting to feel the alcohol. Clyde and Mark asked me when I was going to join the guys. I told them all that this was Kenny and Rudy's gig and they would let me know.

When the first set was over they both came back to our table to join, Mary and Blanche. Kenny smiled and said, "Hank, we will be waving you up to play with us sometime during the next set." I told Kenny that they sounded great. Kenny said, "Thanks, it means a lot coming from you." They finished their beer and headed back to the stage. After about three songs, Kenny waved me to the stage.

We played the rest of the second set together. We all took a break. I then joined them for most of the third set. When I came back to the table just before the end of the third set, I was greeted by all of my friends. They were slapping me on the back and I had a fresh mug of beer waiting.

Ann, Mary, and Mark's wife Jenny were visiting with Mary and Blanche Wait. Ann was telling Blanche that she really enjoyed the showing of her oil paintings last year and said she was looking forward to seeing her charcoals the next day, Sunday. Blanche went on to say that she felt honored to have been invited back for the Art Festival. She said that the Flagstaff Art Festival was one of the most notable art shows in the country. She said that there were always a lot of buyers and famous art critics.

Blanche said, she and Mary, her sister, had just met Kenny and Rudy last night and had such a great time that they looked forward to this evening. Blanche went to the restroom and while she was gone, Mary told us that Blanche was very famous in the Cincinnati area. She said that Blanche had been elected the president of the Cincinnati Art Guild by her fellow artists.

Kenny and Rudy went back to the stage for the final set for the evening. Mary and Blanche stayed with us at our table. We all continued conversing until just before midnight. Mary, my supposed wife, and I finished the last drink and we said goodnight to everyone. Just then Kenny and Rudy came to the table and thanked me for joining them. Kenny said, "You know, Hank, that we are always happy to have you join us anytime we play. You know a group always sounds better when another instrument joins the band."

He asked me if it was possible for us to join them in Mayer for the annual Mayer Days celebration. He said that they would be playing at the dance hall on both Friday and Saturday night. He asked me if I knew the location of the dance hall. I told him, "Of course, it is across the street from the hotel in the strip with the saloon and the country market."

Kenny gave me a little strange look. He said, "Hank, I did not know that you had been to Mayer." I thought to myself, "Many times but when you were older." I told Kenny and Rudy that Mary and I would try to make it up for the weekend. I told him that we were really busy at work but that I would try to get away.

Chapter Five
The Suspect

Just as we started past the bar on our way out, I noticed a gentleman sitting at the bar getting a little loud and obnoxious. As we went by him, Steve said, "That man is Shorty McDonald, and sure enough, he is drinking a beer with his left hand." We all got in the car, and headed back to Flagstaff to their home for the evening.

Seeing Shorty brought to mind the murder case. I asked Steve if we could drop off the ladies and head over to the hotel for just a few moments. He smiled and said, "It sounds like you have further questions with regard to the murder." I told him that it would be after one a.m. by the time we got back to Flagstaff and headed over to the hotel. I told him that I had hoped that we might run into a witness since it would be the same day, Saturday, and the same timeframe.

I told him that I had no proof yet but my gut feeling was that this was not a cold-blooded murder but again a murder of passion. I told him that it might even have been an accident. We dropped the ladies off at the house and headed to the hotel area downtown. I think it was probably somewhere around 1:30 a.m. when we arrived in front of the hotel.

Steve and I stood on the northwest corner of Aspen and Leroux streets. Right in front of us was the hotel Weatherford's front entrance. The hotel actually sat on the southwest corner of the intersection. As we walked around the streets, I was hoping that someone would go by that might have witnessed the incident.

Then as luck would have it, I noticed a man walking across the street coming to the opposite side of Leroux. I hurried across the street in hopes I might intercept him. I stopped him and introduced myself, and then introduced Steve, the Chief of Police. I hoped this might make him feel at ease. I would have been concerned myself if anybody stopped me at 1:30 in the morning.

I then asked him if he worked in the neighborhood. He said that he ran a saloon in the next block east of LeRoux. I asked him if he walked this way on his way home. He said, "Yes, but only Thursday through Sunday, and usually at the same time. Then I asked him if he saw anything out of the ordinary in the past month. I could tell right off that he was feeling a little uncomfortable when talking about the incident.

I sensed that something was wrong. I felt that I needed to make him feel at ease. I mentioned that anything he said would be held in strict confidence. I went on to explain the circumstances surrounding the death of Miss Amy Wilson. I addressed the exact date and asked him again if he saw anything out of the ordinary.

He then admitted that he had seen the whole incident. He said that it was pretty dark, but that he was standing under the street light at the corner, and that there was another light right outside the double doors of the Zane Grey Lounge. He said that he saw the lady come flying out of the double doors of the Zane Grey Lounge on the third level of the Hotel.

He said it looked like she had been pushed or shoved very hard. She hit one of the posts and it appeared to knock her unconscious then she fell backwards over the rail and hit the sidewalk below. He went on to say that he saw a man run out after her just before she hit the post. He was very upset and kept calling her name. He definitely was trying to stop her from falling. He kept yelling her name but she was not able to respond because she was unconscious.

He leaned over the rail and had his head in his hands and was sobbing. I asked him if he recognized the man. He said it was very dark but he said he definitely recognized the man. I asked him if it was Shorty McDonald. He looked a little nervous and then exclaimed that the man was definitely Shorty.

He said that he knew Amy because she worked at the Lounge on the weekends and that often she walked home with him after her weekend shifts. He said that she lived only about a block from him. He said that he also knew Shorty. He said that Shorty had a temper and got a little loud and obnoxious when he drank but generally he was a very gentle soul.

We wrote down his name, Clint Martin, and his phone number, and told him that we would be in touch with him at a later date. We thanked him for his help. Steve gave him his business card and told him that if he thought of any other facts that might be pertinent to solving the case to call him as soon as possible. I guess this must have sparked something in him, because he said that he did see Shorty earlier that same day in his lounge.

Shorty told him that he had a date to walk a lady home after the lounges closed for the night. Clint said that Shorty frequented the bars when he came into town, usually no more than twice a month. He said that he could not remember a time that Shorty got into any scuffle. He was, again, a little obnoxious but generally harmless.

We said good night and then we headed for the barn. I talked to Steve on the ride back to his house. I told him that it not appear to be a cold-blooded murder. The evidence and the witness's statement indicate that Shorty did not mean to kill the girl. He lost his temper and let his emotions get the best of him. Manslaughter would be the most that he was guilty of. I told Steve that we needed to find a way to force Shorty to admit to the crime and tell us the facts.

On the way back to the house, I started thinking that I was probably going to have to sleep with Mary. I felt very uncomfortable with this arrangement but I really did not have much of a choice. We arrived directly, and the girls were sitting on the back porch drinking a glass of wine and talking about the day. Steve went to the icebox and got us both a bottle of beer.

Steve smiled and handed me a beer saying, "Hank, you look a little green again, maybe this beer will settle you down." He went on to ask me if I was having stomach problems again. I told him no and that maybe it was a gas attack. The girls were deep in conversation. I am not sure they even knew that we were there.

I finished the beer and looked over at Mary and said, "Mary, I think that I am going to retire. It has been a long day and I am really tired." I told her to go ahead and enjoy her visit with her sister and that she could go to bed whenever she was through with her visit. I told her not to hurry on my account. I was very nervous about the sleeping arrangement, but the fact was that she thought I was her husband. What would I do if she approached me?

She smiled and said that she would be up a little later. I retired to the bathroom upstairs adjacent to the guest bedroom. I brushed my teeth and changed into a pair of pajamas and headed for bed. I was definitely pooped. It had been an exceptionally long day and I had plenty of beer, that is for sure. The minute my head hit the pillow I was gone.

Some time later I was awakened by the woman who was next to me in bed and obviously in a romantic mood. I was half-asleep, and confused. The woman kissed me, and in my dream-like state, I was kissing Rose. Part of me knew it was Mary, but all I could think about Rose, and in my heart I was with her. I felt very strange. I wondered if this was adultery. It was a very confusing situation. I immediately fell back asleep after the encounter. I woke up early the next morning and still was feeling guilty. I just was not sure if I had done anything wrong.

Mary gave me a big hug and smiled. She said that she had never experienced such an encounter before and suggested that beer obviously was the drink of the future as far as she was concerned. I looked at her and smiled all the while thinking, "Are you kidding me, at some point she would have this guy Hank back in her life." I did not have the heart to tell her the truth and she probably would not have believed it anyway.

Chapter Six
Back to Phoenix

We both finished dressing. We finished packing our bags and headed down stairs to the kitchen. Steve and Ann were already at the table. They both had a cup of coffee and Steve was reading the morning paper. Ann had made ham and cheese omelets. We finished our breakfast and enjoyed another cup of coffee.

Steve told me that he would get back to me with regard to the investigation. He said that he had thought about the situation and that he felt that, in fact, the evidence supported an accidental death. I told them that I had really enjoyed the weekend and was glad that I was able to help solve the case. We all hugged and Steve reminded me that they expected to see us again next weekend for the big party at Yarnell Hill. We waved goodbye as we pulled away.

Mary and I stopped at the Union 76 station to fill up the car. One tank of gas would get us all the way home. Our car got twenty-five miles to the gallon. The gas was five cents per gallon. Our tank held fifteen gallons. It cost sixty cents to fill the tank to the brim with gasoline. I remember filling up the new car just the other morning and it cost twenty-five dollars. It was just hard to believe that now gas was only five cents a gallon.

Mary picked up the Sunday morning edition of the Arizona Republic newspaper, which was ten cents. She expressed a complaint stating that she thought that they should charge the same for the Sunday edition as the weekly edition, which was five cents. I told her that there were usually more sales ads in the Sunday edition and for most women this made their day. I smiled and told her that she was not like most women, being that the ads did not interest her. She smiled back at me and we headed south toward Phoenix on the Old Black Canyon Highway. I looked down at my watch and the time was 9:05 a.m. I figured it would take us just under six hours to get home traveling at twenty-five miles per hour, so we could plan on getting home about 2:00 p.m.

I wasn't sure where home was but I knew it was somewhere in the Phoenix area. I got a little nervous as we passed the Stoneman Lake exit, thinking about the circumstances on the way up and knowing that this was the exact place where the excitement all began. The weather was clear and sunny, not a cloud in the sky.

We arrived in Phoenix at 2 p.m. I continued down the highway and just as I was passing Roosevelt, Mary hollered at me, "Hank, where are you going." I said, "Sorry, I must have been daydreaming." I turned left on Roosevelt hoping this was the correct street. I continued east on Roosevelt, and then sure enough right at the corner of Fifth street and Roosevelt, I saw a beautiful home with the name Smelser on the sign out front.

Underneath the Smelser name appeared our first names, Hank and Mary. I pulled in the driveway of a beautiful Victorian style home and parked in the covered carport. It was a beautiful home with a well manicured grass front lawn. Mary laughed and said, "Hank, thank God, you did not forget where we live. I smiled all the while thinking, "Are you kidding me? I just got lucky."

I unloaded our luggage and headed up the porch to the front door, following Mary. As she unlocked the front door, I thought to myself, "Business must be good, whatever business I was in." Mary must have read my mind. She said, "My parents would have been very proud of you Hank. You did a great job in painting the old house and replacing the wood floors."

She went on to say that she was very thankful that they left this house to us, but was happy that they left their house in

Flagstaff to Steve and Ann. Well, at least I knew how we could afford this beautiful home. Mary picked up our copy of the Sunday paper and said, "Well, Hank we can both read the same sections today since we have two papers." We proceeded to the master bedroom, which was on the main floor.

After unpacking, we headed to the kitchen. Mary asked if I was hungry. I told her I was. She went to the icebox and pulled out part of a roast of beef and a package of fresh cheddar cheese. I went right over to the breadbox and pulled out half a loaf of what looked like some type of wheat bread. Mary smiled and said that she had gotten the loaf from Karsh's bakery.

She put the roast on a cutting board and sliced it into thin slices. She loaded the sandwiches with sprouts, tomatoes and lettuce. She put the sandwiches on plates and then poured herself a glass of wine and gave me a bottle of beer. She smiled and said, "The bottle has been in the icebox a couple of weeks. Lucky for you Steve left one here the last time they were here." I smiled and said, "Thanks, I will totally enjoy this bottle of beer with the sandwich."

We both headed for the front porch and sat in a couple of rocking chairs with a table between us that would hold our plates and our beverages. We finished our sandwiches and beverage, and Mary reached over, put tobacco in a pipe, and handed it to me. It was obvious that she had done this many times before. I lit the pipe and we both sat on the porch reading the paper and discussing various articles.

We also discussed the events of the weekend and both agreed that it was a very relaxing weekend considering all of the odd events. A thought rushed through my head. I was an asthmatic and I wondered what I would do if I had an attack. I then asked Mary how they handled an asthma attack. She looked at me with a very strange look. She said, "Where the hell did that come from, asthma." I told her that I had read about the disease and wondered how it was treated.

She said that usually the fire department is called and they put the victim in an oxygen tent. I just thanked her for the information. She said that she could not believe with all of my detective knowledge, that I did not know the facts about to asthma. I said, "Oh well, whatever." I definitely felt a little more at ease.

Mary went on to say that she and Ann had decided to refer sewing jobs to each other. Ann had met several new customers in her seamstress shop in Flagstaff, who lived in Phoenix and wanted her to refer them to a good seamstress in Phoenix. Mary, in turn, said that she would refer business to Ann. They both figured that it would work out well in the long run.

The time just seemed to fly by and when I looked down at my watch, it was 8:30 p.m. Mary said that she was going to go in and take a shower and ready herself to retire for the evening. I told her that I would be in after little while. I hoped that she would be asleep by the time I went to bed. I still was feeling uncomfortable with this whole situation.

I think about forty-five minutes went by and I started to yawn. I knew it was time to retire. I headed in the house and locked both the front and back door and then went to the master bath. As I passed by our room I noticed Mary was in bed already, but was reading a book. I went in the bathroom and took a shower myself and after drying myself off, I slipped into clean pajamas and got into bed. All the while Mary continued reading her book. I thought to myself, "Great, this may work."

I turned my head away from her and then the next thing I felt was her body up against me, hugging me. I just could not understand how she did not know that I was not her husband. Well, it really did not matter, because as soon as I closed my eyes and her lips touched mine, I felt I was holding Rose in my arms. Mary fell asleep immediately afterwards, and I lay there thinking of Rose, feeling strangely close to her. I wondered if she could feel me close to her too.

Chapter Seven
Smelser Investigations

The alarm went off at 6:30 a.m. I struggled getting out of bed. I headed to the bathroom to drain the dew off my lily. I came back and stood in front of the mirror over our bedroom dresser. Mary was still asleep. I was about to take a shower and I was thinking to myself, "This is great. Here I am and I do not have a clue where I'm going."

Just then the Lord answered my prayer. I looked down at the top of the dresser and there was a business card. The card said, "Hank Smelser Investigations." On the back of the card was written what I specialized in, auto accident and workers comp investigations. My office was in the Luhrs Tower on the southeast corner of Central Avenue and Jefferson in downtown Phoenix. It was on the 5th floor, Suite 510. Luckily I know the city, so I knew right where it was located.

I finished washing up and picked out a sports shirt, gabardine pants, argyle socks, and black dress shoes. As I started to walk out of the bedroom, Mary called to me, "Hank, wait a minute, I need a hug to get me started for today." I stopped and she came up and hugged me. She told me that she loved me, and said she would make sure we never ran out of beer.

I just smiled, not understanding, her thoughts, but it sounded great to always have a cold one in the icebox. She smiled and said, "Hank, why aren't you wearing a shirt and tie as usual." I told her I wanted to relax a little. She smiled again and said, "I like the new Hank." I thought, "Yeah, I bet you do." I was amazed that I was pulling this whole identity situation off.

I waved goodbye, and on the way out the back door, I poured myself a cup of last night's coffee. I then realized that there was no microwave to heat up the coffee. I took the cup of cold coffee and headed for the carport. I asked myself one question? How did these people exist without a microwave oven? How did I exist prior to our first microwave oven?

I got into the car and got ready to start the car. I looked out at the passenger side rear view mirror to be sure that I was not too close to the van. I noticed the writing on the side of the panel truck that read Mary's Stitch Shop. The address and phone number were also displayed on the side of the panel truck. I thought to myself that Mary must be a successful business owner.

I backed down the driveway and made sure that the street was clear of traffic. I then headed south on Fifth Street toward downtown Phoenix. I parked out front on the street and headed up to my office. I tried all of the keys I had until I found the right key. Heck, I had never been in this office and had no clue which key was the right one.

I finally found the right key and was about to open the door when I heard a soft woman's voice say "Hank, is that you?" I answered yes, and she opened the door." The young lady had a smile on her face. I did not know what to say because I had never seen this woman. I looked over at the desk and saw the name Keri Sanford. I took a chance and said, "Good morning Keri." She said good morning back and then asked, "What was with the door situation?" I told her that I was half asleep.

Keri asked me how the weekend went and brought me a cup of hot coffee. After drinking the cold cup from home, this was a pleasant change. Hot coffee, what a concept, seems logical. She asked me how Mary was doing and if we had a good weekend. I said both Mary and the weekend were great. I went to the back office just assuming it was my office.

I had only been seated a minute or two when Keri handed me a stack of messages. She said, "Hank, we have a busy week ahead of us." She appeared to be a very organized individual. She then asked how the investigation of the evidence went with regard to the Amy Wilson death. Her statement reminded me that I needed to see what I could find out about the suspect.

I asked her to contact Washington and get all the information she could on a person named Shorty McDonald. I told her that all I knew was that he was a ranch hand on the Fox Ranch, and that he had once ridden with the Cowboys out of Tombstone, just before they were disbanded. Keri said, "I'll get on the telegraph and see what I can find out about this Shorty McDonald."

She reached over the desk and pulled out a file from the stack. It was the most pressing case. She said that it was a worker's comp investigation. As I read through the file, I noted that the claimant had suffered a lower back injury, and was unable to perform his construction job. He had been out of work for two months.

The insurance company wanted my firm to investigate the claimant to be sure that he was legitimate. I took the file and told Keri that I was going to pay a visit to the man. The State of Arizona enacted the Worker's Compensation branch of the State government in 1925. They were still in the growing stage and were under-staffed, so they hired my firm to do their investigations. I gathered evidence and submitted my results to the Work Comp Bureau, and they settled claims according to my gathered evidence. It was not very exciting work, but it paid the bills and the work was steady.

The claimant's name was Paul Edring. I grabbed the file and headed out to see this person. Surprising him might prove to be beneficial. I thought that if I observed him for a while, I might discover whether or not he was actually injured. The State of Arizona, our client, suspected that he might be ready to return to work. The Edring farm was located out in

West Phoenix at 75th Avenue and Buckeye Roads. This was in the southwest part of the city. It was about ten miles from downtown Phoenix.

While driving out there, I could not quit thinking about the Amy Wilson death case in Flagstaff. All of the facts and evidence kept going through my mind. I kept coming up with the same scenario. The evidence, investigation, and statements kept pointing to an accidental death. I arrived near the Edring farm and pulled over onto the shoulder of the road. I could see the front and back of the home. I sat there drinking my coffee for at least forty-five minutes watching for any movement.

Finally, I noticed a male come out of the front door. He walked across the front yard, which was very large. He definitely was walking with a grimace on his face. He went to the mailbox and collected their mail and headed back to the house. He stopped for a minute, and bent over just a little with his hands on his knees. I knew then that this guy was for real, if it was in fact Paul Edring.

I started the car after he went into the house, and pulled forward entering the property via the circular driveway. I stopped in front of the house. I got out of my car, and with the file in hand, went up to the front door and knocked. The door opened and a lady in her forties said, "Good Afternoon." I introduced myself, and said that I represented the State with regard to the workers compensation claim for Paul Edring. I asked if I had the right home and that I just needed to talk to Mr. Edring to clear up some facts regarding his disability claim.

She said, "Yes, you are in the right home." She pointed over to the couch in the living room and there sat the man that I saw going out to get the mail. She spoke and said, "Paul, honey, this gentleman is here to see you." He put the mail down and I could see that he had a heating pad around his back. She smiled and said to me, "Poor Paul, he can't even walk to the mailbox without experiencing pain." She said he had been laid up for almost two months and was recovering, but very slowly.

I told him not to get up and I extended my hand. He shook my hand and thanked me for not having to get up. He asked me to sit in the chair next to him and proceed with any questions that might come to me. He introduced himself as Paul Edring, and then introduced his wife, Marguerite. She said, "Marg for short." I spent the next half hour gathering the facts about his injury, and we discussed his medical treatment.

I told him it was against the rules for me to make any suggestions, but I told him that with a lower back injury that there was a chance that a bone specialist could help him with his injury. I told him that the State of Arizona would pay for the treatments. I went on to explain that I was under contract with the state to help them with workers compensation claims. It was up to me to either validate or negate any claim.

It was obvious that Mr. Edring was in a lot of pain. I said I would get in touch with the doctor in to secure all of the medical information. I told them everything would be okay, not to worry.

I shook hands with both of them and then I told Mr. Edring that I hoped he would recover soon because I could see that the injury was driving him crazy, being housebound and not being able to work. They both smiled and thanked me for the visit

Chapter Eight
Dissolution of the Case

I arrived back at my office in the Luhrs Tower. I waved to Keri and headed back to my office. She was on the phone, but put the person on hold to tell me that she had received information regarding Shorty, and it was on the top of my desk. I went over the report about Shorty. The report from Washington indicated that Shorty did not have a criminal record.

I then wondered how this could be if he rode with the lawless Cowboy gang out of Tombstone. The report indicated that he was with the gang right before they were disbanded, and that he actually never rode with them. He became a ranch hand, and moved to the Flagstaff area in the late 1800's.

After reading his profile, I was fairly sure he was not a murderer. He was guilty of stretching the truth. He was definitely a bullshit artist. The fact that he lied about his past put a damper on the current incident, and he probably felt he would not be treated fairly if he confessed. I knew there had to be a way to get him to talk.

After reviewing the report again, I picked up the phone and called Steve. The first thing Steve mentioned was that the witness came into the police station. After looking at several pictures, the witness said there was no doubt that the individual he saw on the balcony just before the lady went over was Shorty McDonald. Steve also said that he was picking up a warrant for the arrest of Shorty for murder.

I told Steve not to jump the gun. I told him that Shorty had no previous criminal record, and that this was the first crime that he had ever committed. I told him absolutely that it was an accident. I said the only thing Shorty was guilty of was losing his temper and pushing the lady through the double doors. I told Steve that from that point on, it was just a set of accidental circumstances that led to her death.

I told him that I had a plan, and that I thought that if we could get around this guy that the truth would come out. I told him that Mary and I had plans to meet them in Mayer for the Mayer Days Celebration. Maybe Shorty would be there and we could execute my plan.

Steve said that he had gone to the Fox Ranch looking for Shorty. The owner, Mr. Fox, told Steve that Shorty seemed very distraught about something that had happened, and that he took a week off to be with his family in Yarnell. Mr. Fox mentioned that Shorty planned to attend the Mayer Days Celebration on his way back to the ranch the next week. Steve said that everything that I had told him made sense.

I told him that Shorty was not running out. He was simply scared to come forward knowing that he had created a problem bragging about his past. I told Steve that we had already made reservations at the hotel for Friday and Saturday night. I assured Steve that I was willing to play my hunch. I told him that I believed that if confronted with the crime, Shorty would not be violent.

Steve said he would go along with me unless he saw trouble brewing. I told him, "Fine, I'll play by your rules." The week seemed to fly by and it was already Friday. Keri hurried me out of the office at 3 p.m. She said that she had spoken with Mary, and that we had reservations for dinner with Steve and Ann at 6 p.m. at the steakhouse. I left the office early and sure enough, when I arrived, Mary already had our bags packed for the weekend.

Mary was definitely a good cook, but she couldn't compare to my Rose's cooking. Nevertheless, I told her that I was looking forward to meeting Steve and Ann for dinner, but that I would miss her cooking. Hank and Mary had no children, so it was a lot easier to prepare for just two, I guess. I thought of Rose again, and our family. I really missed Rose, and our children.

Each night after dinner, Mary and I would sit on the front porch and listen to the radio. She always made sure that I had a cold beer and that my pipe was ready. I read the paper each night, and Mary would occupy her time by completing the crossword puzzles. It was hard for me to believe that this was the same town that I was raised in many years later. It was all hustle and bustle in the future, and not as relaxing as this era. Nevertheless I wished I could have my hustling, bustling family back again.

I put our bags in the trunk and Mary locked the house. We headed for the Blakely Gas Station and filled up for the trip. We got out of town by 3:30, which would allow us to be in Mayer before 6 p.m. As we left town, Mary mentioned that Keri was a very good secretary. She said, "I called Keri on Tuesday and informed her that we needed to leave early on Friday. She said that she would schedule your appointments to free you up by then." Keri did her job well.

I agreed, "Before leaving for the day, Keri told me she spoke with the Workman's Compensation office. They were satisfied with the legitimacy of the Edring claim. She told me that they were going to pay his medical bills, and start sending the weekly income checks the next Friday. I called the claims manager and thanked him for moving so quickly on this matter. He said that he never doubted my investigations in the past and was not about to start now."

I told Mary that I told the claims manager that these folks were in bad financial shape and that they needed the money. He thanked me and told me that I could come by and pick up my fee. He said that he had several new cases for me to work.

I told Mary that Keri hurried me out of the office at 2 p.m. I paid her for the week, and was very surprised to see the balance in the checkbook. It was almost two thousand dollars. Keri handed me two hundred dollars. She said that she had drawn this out at Mary's instructions so that we would have funds for the weekend.

Mary said that she completed two wedding dresses and both clients picked them up before noon. She was able to get home early enough to pack clothes for the trip. I guess there are some advantages to not having any children. You can come and go as you please. I still missed the family life. There is a lot of action going on with a big family, that is for sure. This was a totally different lifestyle.

I thanked Mary for packing my bag, and we headed down the road. We arrived in Mayer at 5:40 p.m. that evening. I noticed when signing in that Kenny and Rudy, my musical buddies, were already out on the town. The deskman smiled and told Mary and me that Kenny and Rudy were at the Bordello.

I also noticed that Steve and Ann had also checked into the hotel. The deskman told us that Steve and Ann were already seated at the restaurant. We went upstairs and unpacked our bags and then headed across the street. Mary spoke about Kenny and Rudy as we crossed the street, stating that they were really a pair of crazy dudes. I smiled and said, "Hey, that is Kenny and Rudy, nobody is going to change them." I told her that these two had a ton of energy. We walked through the front door and there were Steve and Ann.

Steve stood up and shook my hand. Ann stood up and she and Mary hugged. We sat down and ordered the house specialty, which was chicken fried steak, mashed potatoes and green beans. While we waited for the dinner to be served the girls were engulfed in conversation about the seamstress business.

Steve just could not hold back. Steve told us that Mary and Blanche, the two ladies that we met at Mormon Lake Lodge, were in town for the big party.

He said that Blanche had won several awards for her oil paintings and her charcoals. He went on to say that she sold several pieces and she was very happy with the exhibit. He said that they were on their way back to Phoenix to catch the train to return to Cincinnati.

He then started talking about Shorty. Right after dinner Steve ordered a shot of Jack Daniels for each of us. He said that he and Ann spoke with Kenny and Rudy, and that they were expecting me to join them again for a couple of music sets. He said that Mary and Blanche did not know the whereabouts of Kenny and Rudy. Kenny and Rudy did not know that the ladies were in town and he asked us to keep the situation to ourselves.

We had another shot and had a toast to the celebration and the companionship. The time just seemed to fly by and lo and behold it was time to go next door to the dance palace to meet the boys as they set up for the evening gig. We got a table and Mary ordered a beer for Steve and myself, and a mixed drink for the ladies.

She ordered a rum and coke for herself and for Ann. We just finished the first round when Kenny and Rudy walked into the dance hall. They waved toward our table and headed to set up on the stage. About twenty minutes later, Mary and Blanche entered the dance palace and joined us at our table. The place started to fill up early and was packed by 8 pm.

There were a lot of people in town for the celebration. The boys started the first set right at about 8:30, and the party was on in full swing. We danced to several songs in that first set and the dance floor was already packed. The guys called me to the stage in the middle of the second set, and we rocked with some of our favorite songs.

I finished the second set with them and they asked me if I was going to join them for the third set. I told them that I had a long day and that I was pretty tired. I told them that I knew that Saturday would be a barnburner and that I needed to rest up for the evening festivities. Mary and I had one more drink during the third set, and then said goodnight to Steve, Ann, and Blanche.

I waved to the guys on the stage as we started walking out of the dance palace. On the way out, I overheard a couple of cowboys that were at he bar. They mentioned that they expected Shorty to join them for the evening festivities. One mentioned to the other that Shorty had been in Yarnell with his family. He said that Shorty had experienced some sort of problem and that he needed to sort everything out.

Chapter Nine
Shorty McDonald

Mary and I both woke up almost at the same time the next morning, Saturday. I went to the bathroom first. I took a shower, brushed my teeth, and combed my hair. When I got out of the bathroom, Mary was waiting. She told me to be patient, and that they had complimentary coffee and a morning paper downstairs at the front desk. She asked me to go down and get the newspaper and bring her back a cup of coffee with cream and sugar.

I decided to take her advice and went downstairs to get our complimentary coffee and the paper. I brought them back to the room and proceeded to read the paper and enjoy the cup of coffee. Mary did not take long getting ready. We were both dressed and headed across the street for breakfast by 7 a.m.

After breakfast we took a walk around the town. We both really loved Mayer, and had considered a second home somewhere in the town or the surrounding area. We met a couple of realtors at breakfast and they gave us a map of the listings in the area and told us to call either of them if we had any questions. We were able to see all of the listings we were interested in by driving to the different properties.

The time seemed to fly by and before we knew it was 3:30 p.m. We had been so engrossed looking at the homes for sale that we missed lunch. Steve and Ann had left for the restaurant for dinner. We were to meet them and the rest of the Flagstaff gang at Reatta Pass Steak house just this side of Humboldt. It was the next town about seven miles south and east of Prescott.

We were all excited because an early dinner was just what we needed since we both missed lunch. Perfect, we both thought. We arrived at about four p.m. and joined Steve, Ann and the rest of the gang. Steve took the liberty of ordering a beer for all of the men. He ordered a glass of wine for Mary and Ann.

Ann smiled at Mary, and asked her if she had a headache from the festivities from the prior evening. Ann said she was going to take it easy tonight. Mary smiled and said, "Yes, I needed a couple of aspirin this morning, but I am feeling great right now."

The waitress came back with our drinks and then asked us if we were ready to place our dinner order. It is pretty obvious that when you are at a steakhouse you order steaks. Steve and I ordered a 12 oz T-bone steak, cowboy beans, and a baked potato. The girls ordered the 8 oz Delmonico with the same trimmings. This steakhouse was famous for mesquite wood barbeque steaks. We finished dinner at about six pm.

We all got up and headed to the dance palace which was right down the street. We walked in and headed for our table, which was already occupied by our friends. I noticed Shorty at the end of the bar as we walked by on the way to our table. We all said hello and sat down at the table.

I told Steve that I wanted to talk with Shorty. Steve said, "Be my guest." I headed over to Shorty and sat right next to him. I ordered a beer and offered to by him a beer. I extended my hand and introduced myself as an old west historian. I told him that I heard that he once rode with the Cowboy gang from Tombstone. He accepted the drink and said he would be glad to shed some light on the gang.

He was very open, and proceeded to tell me his story. "My older brother was one of the original members of the Cowboys, having been recruited by Curly Bill himself. My brother was killed in a scuffle with another one of the Cowboys. I quit the gang to get the man who killed my brother."

Shorty went on, "I was only with the gang a couple of months. Then I found out that my brother's killer had been shot down right after the Corral incident. I knew that it was the end of the Cowboys because the Earps swore that they would all die. So I headed north out of Tombstone and did not stop until I ran out of water, money and food. That's how

I ended up here at the Fox Ranch, and I've been working here ever since. I guess I've gotten a reputation because I rode with the Cowboys, but truthfully, it's pretty exaggerated."

Since I had him talking I asked him if he knew Amy Wilson. He looked at me and had a tear in his eye. He answered me, "I was there with her the night that she died. We had quarreled because I was jealous of a patron who was talking with her. She came over to try to explain that she was just doing her job. She then accused me of having an affair with a local hairdresser."

Shorty told me that he lost his temper right then and there. He wiped away a tear with his sleeve and said, "I grabbed her arm and swung her, and she went backwards through the double doors on the balcony outside the Zane Grey Room. She hit her head against one of the poles. I chased after her, but she was knocked out when she hit the pole and she fell backwards. I was an arm length from her when she went over the rail."

He was sobbing now as he told me that he ran from the scene because he felt with his reputation, he would not be treated fairly. Steve, overhearing the conversation, came up and arrested Shorty without any trouble. It was obvious that Shorty was remorseful. He told us both that he was glad that it was over, and that he could not live with himself after the death of this woman that he loved.

I told him that he would get a fair trial, and that all of the evidence pointed to the fact that the death was definitely not premeditated. Steve handcuffed Shorty and took him to the Mayer Jail. Steve said he would be transporting him back to Flagstaff to stand trial. Steve came back to the restaurant about a half hour later. We discussed the case again and he thanked me for helping him.

I told him that I expected to testify at the trial, and that I hoped that the jury would go easy on Shorty. Steve told me that he was going to suggest that Shorty be tried for manslaughter. He felt that when he went over all of the evidence and testimonies that the judge would see the truth.

We finished our drinks just as Kenny and Rudy finished the second set. I told them what had occurred and told them that I was sorry that I could not join them for some tunes. They told me no problem and that they understood. They both assured me that there would be many more opportunities in the future. We said good night to Kenny, Rudy, Blanche and Ann, and said we were heading for the barn, so to speak.

Steve and Ann said that they were going to stay for a little longer. They said would meet us for breakfast before we all headed back home. Mary and I both crashed upon hitting the bed. I knew for sure that it had been a long day, because Mary fell asleep before me. I was also spent and was very glad that she fell asleep, so I did not have to worry about any funny business.

Chapter Ten
The Fog Lifts

We woke the next morning early. We took our turns taking a shower. We got dressed, packed our bags, and then headed downstairs for breakfast. As we passed the front desk, we met Steve and Ann. We all walked across the street to the restaurant. We enjoyed our breakfast together and we discussed the weekend events.

Steve said that he and Ann would be taking Shorty back with them and that they would keep us in the loop. We finished breakfast, then we all rose from the table, hugged, and shook hands. Mary and I went back to the hotel to get our bags and check out. Steve and Ann headed for the town jail to pick up Shorty. Mary decided to drive us home, so after loading our bags, I got into the passenger side of the car and we left Mayer and headed to Phoenix.

I think we were only a couple of miles down the road when I fell asleep. I do not know how much time passed but I felt a nudge, and I woke up and there driving the car was Rose. I must have looked astonished because she smiled and said, "Tom, are you okay?" I told her no, I looked up in the rearview mirror and sure enough it was me, Tommy. I can't believe it, I am in our new Explorer and the sun is shining and it is beautiful outside.

I asked Rose to stop for a minute. After she pulled off the road I got out and walked to the front of the car. I had to sort this whole situation out, but I was glad that I was back where I belonged. After I walked around for a couple of minutes to clear my head and gather my thoughts, I came back to the front of the car where Rose was standing. She looked at me with the strangest smile and said again, "Tommy, are you all right?" I was so choked up to see her again, that all I could do was look at her and say, "I think so."

I looked down at my watch and it was three o'clock. I guess we had been off the road for a couple of hours. We stood there for a few moments and Rose began to tell me that I had fallen asleep shortly after we pulled off the road. She said that the fog was so thick that she could not see five feet in front of her, and that she decided to wait it out before proceeding. She said it was so bad that she could not even see the front of the hood on the new Explorer.

Then she asked me, "Do you have any idea what you were dreaming about?" At first I could not say anything. Then I really told a good lie, I said to her, "I have no clue." Rose went on to say, "Tommy, you were mumbling, laughing and had some of the most serious looks on your face that I have never ever seen. A couple of times you had the most shit eating grin on your face. What was that all about?"

I said, "Honey I have no idea." I said it kind of sheepishly and she gave me one of her looks of disbelief. I broke up the conversation and told her, "Come on honey, we are late and the boys will be worried. She said, "Ok, but I sure wish I could read that devious mind of yours." I laughed and said, "Honey, it was a dream. What more can I say? Besides, I can't remember what I was dreaming about. I don't know about you but I do not remember dreams after I wake up."

She smiled and said, "Well, you are right about not remembering dreams because I can't ever remember what I dreamed about after I wake up." In my mind I patted myself on the back for getting out of that one, but I could not keep Hank, Mary, and the rest of them out of my mind.

A few years later I was at my father-in-law's house for dinner. He mentioned that he had a friend coming over that he had just met recently on a music gig. He had invited him over to practice a few songs for a job at the VFW post in two weeks. He mentioned that this fellow was quite a bit older than him, but he said this guy was one hell of a banjo player. He dropped the subject and I did not give it another thought.

We had a great dinner. My mother-in-law is an incredible cook. After dinner we were in the back yard having a beer. I heard the doorbell and a few minutes later my father-in-law came to the back yard and got our attention. He said, "Tommy, I want you to meet my friend Rudy." I was speechless.

There standing in front of me was a man that looked to be in his eighties. It definitely was Rudy Mac. I couldn't talk. My father-in-law looked at me and said, "Tommy, are you all right? You look like you just saw a ghost." I still didn't say anything. He then said, "Rudy, I would like you to meet my son-in-law, Tommy."

Rudy extended his hand and I shook his hand. I finally spoke and said to Rudy, "Are you Rudy Mac, who used to play banjo with Kenny Harris, the fiddle player?" I could see now it was Rudy who was at a loss for words. He looked at me and said, "Do I know you?" I smiled and said, "I think so, I am little Tommy." He broke out laughing and said, "You're little Tommy?" I said, "You bet! It is me."

We spent the next hour talking about old times and all of the hunting trips that we all shared. The conversation was strictly about hunting and music. We never discussed the other activities that he and Kenny pursued while on those trips. Finally I got around to asking Rudy, "Do you remember the trip to Mayer when you guys introduced me to Hank Smelser?"

He said, "Yes I do, that was the time that Kenny and I worked very late that Friday night. Hank volunteered to take you hunting that next morning. We needed to rest because we had another gig on Saturday night." I laughed to myself because he really pushed the fact that they played late that

Friday. He had a twinkle in his eye and I said, "Yeah, at the boarding house." Then we both laughed.

I said, "Rudy, Hank told me a story while we were out hunting that day about a case that he and his brother-in-law Steve worked on. He said Steve was the chief of police in Flagstaff, and they were investigating the death of a teacher, Amy Wilson. He told me that the suspect's name was Shorty McDonald. Did they ever solve that murder case? Do you know if they arrested Shorty for the murder? " I went on to ask him if the case went to a trial. And if so, did he know the final verdict?

Rudy said, "Tom, if I remember correctly, I don't believe Shorty was convicted and the case was closed and considered an accident." Rudy said, "Why do you ask?" I told him that Hank had been telling me the story while we were out hunting. Hank never finished the story because, when we got back to the hotel, his wife Mary was waiting for us. She told him that he needed to hurry to get ready for his gig. Sadly, I never saw Hank again, so I never did get the rest of the story.

Rudy had a look of bewilderment and said, "Strange that you should remember Shorty McDonald. That whole incident occurred in the early 1930's and all of the principles are dead except me." He said he and Kenny were really not involved in the case. He said he did remember the circumstances. "Kenny and I heard Steve and Hank discussing the case one weekend while we played a gig at Mormon Lake Lodge."

I looked at him, smiled and said, "It was just one of those kid memories that has bothered me over the years." I looked up at him and saw that Rudy Mac puzzled look and I thought to myself, "If you only knew what I remembered, you would shit right here." But I figured that he had heard enough for one night.

I saw Rudy from time to time after that evening because he and my father-in-law did several gigs over the next four years. I met his wife and for some reason I did not remember her. My mother-in-law, Val, said that she would sing along with the guys while they were playing with a trilling voice like a bird. In any event one of us came up with a label for her, "Bird Woman." I could see why Rudy could not wait to get away when he was younger. .

The amazing thing was that every time I saw Rudy after that first meeting, he would always have that shit eating grin, and I always had the same grin. I knew that he was aware that I knew the whole story about those trips, but we kept the stories to ourselves. He passed away about five years after we met at my in-laws home. I never told him about my visit to his earlier life.

INTO THE DARK

Into the Dark
By

Zeke Crandall
March 8, 2001

Dedicated to
Keith Parks

Chapter One
The Copperopolis Mine

It was the first Friday of September of 1979. My old boss Keith called and said that we were headed to a mine north of Castle Hot Springs. The resort had burned down for the second time in 1976. Jim, Keith's friend, was going with us and we were excited because he was a licensed geologist and had a blasting license. He had been able to attain the mineral rights of an abandoned gold mine. We only had the rights to the quartz shale that was lying near the crushing plant at the mine.

I was up early Saturday morning and headed over to Keith's house. He had the coffee on when I arrived. He poured me a cup and pulled out the morning paper and a topographical map of the area where we were headed. He pointed out the financial page and showed me where silver was $45 per ounce and gold was $600 per ounce.

We grabbed our cups of coffee and got into his 1966 Ford Bronco. He said that Jim had just picked up his new 1979 Ford four-wheel drive truck and had loaded it and was meeting us at the Lake Pleasant road turnoff on the west side of the lake. He explained that at $600 per ounce the shale was worth something if we could get the quartz to the crushing plant. In the old days the miners only worked the veins, where they could see the gold and left the shale.

Pretty logical since the gold was worth $35 per ounce then, but now the gold that could not be seen by the naked eye was worth something. When we got there Jim explained that along with the gold in the quartz there was silver and mercury. He said that we would load the truck and haul it to the assay office in Wickenburg and he felt we could make some money and have some fun. As long as gold was $600 per ounce it would be worth our work.

It was probably about 7 a.m. when we met Jim, and I noticed Jim had four cases of beer in the back of the truck. He had a mouth full of Copenhagen chewing tobacco. I never saw a man in my life that could drink beer like Jim. He drank a half case from the time we left the turnoff until we arrived at Castle Hot Springs, which was only about five miles from the meeting place. He kept the back window of the truck open for discarding the empties in the back of the truck.

Even more amazing was the fact that you would never have known that he had a drink unless you actually saw him drinking the beer. The guy was like a camel. Jim was about six foot tall, weighed about 170 lbs and had a black handlebar mustache. He still seemed fine when got to the resort, about five miles from the end of the paved Lake Pleasant road. Jim definitely knew a lot of about Arizona history. He was a true cowboy in every sense of the word. He was born in Arizona and had done some mining before he got his blasting and geology licenses. He graduated from NAU with a geology degree.

As we sat on the tailgate of Jim's truck in front of the resort I noticed that the back of the truck was loaded with equipment. He had a whole case of chemicals that he used to determine the ores that were present in the quartz. We sat there for about forty-five minutes while Jim explained that the resort had been a hot spot around the turn of the century.

Jim said the resort was famous because the hot water that came out of the springs was very high in sulfur content. He said the water was considered to have great healing powers and had attracted many celebrities including Clark Gable, Lana Turner and John Wayne. He said that the resort burned the first time in 1956 and they rebuilt the resort. Then it burned again in the early 1970's. He said that there was a grease fire in the kitchen of the main building.

The building was four stories high and made of hollow concrete block with a stucco finish. There were three other buildings on the property. They were Victorian style homes. The place looked terrible, completely in shambles. We wandered around the property for a while and Jim explained a lot about the place. What was hard to believe was that this place was one of the elite hot spots in Arizona for many years. It was amazing that this place could be out in the middle of nowhere.

We drove another 5 miles or more down the Castle Creek wash past the resort. We finished our coffee and headed north on the west side of the resort. I guess we had driven about three more miles and then we took a side trail that headed north of the Creek bed. I really mean it when I say it was a trail. We always traveled with two vehicles just as a precaution in case one of us got stuck. We drove up that road about another mile or so and then turned west down into a wash. Then we could see that there was another trail.

I can't believe that they took those trails in buckboards and prairie schooners. It was tough riding for us and we were in four-wheel drive vehicles with huge knobby off road tires. Imagine how hard it must have been for the pioneer folks. We had air conditioning and windows. Those poor folks had nothing but dust and heat.

We arrived at our destination about two hours later. The mine was surprisingly in great condition, considering that it had not been worked in over sixty years. The main shaft had the big tower over it with the original pulleys still on it. Jim explained that they used the pulleys and buckets to bring up the ore to the surface. At the surface there was a rail track from the tower to the crushing plant, which was about one hundred yards southwest of the mine.

Jim was standing beside a mountain of quartz shale below the crushing plant that extended about seventy feet down the mountain and probably about one hundred feet across. I never saw so much quartz in my life. As I was wandering around the outside of the mine I found a side shaft. Jim explained that there were always several side shafts for escape in case a problem occurred in the main shaft. He was definitely a wealth of knowledge.

Jim took out his box of chemicals he began to test the quartz shale for gold content. He said the ore contained a higher than normal content of gold and mercury. He said it would it would definitely be worth our effort. I found several broken bottles lying around the mine site. They were real thick and looked very old. Jim explained that they stopped working the mine in the early nineteen hundreds. I was really amazed because it looked like the workers had just left the mine the day before.

We loaded up the truck with the quartz and headed for the crushing plant and assay office in Wickenburg, about twenty-four miles away. At least it was a decent road from the mine to Wickenburg. We arrived in there at 11 a.m. and unloaded the ore. The manager of the assay office ran the ore through the crushing plant and about an hour later he gave us a break down of the ore with the amount of each mineral found. We had gold, silver and mercury. He gave us a check for $2100. I could not believe it. Jim cut both Keith and me a check for $700 each. It was not easy money but it really was fun.

Well, that was our part time job for the next few months. Every weekend, we would meet at Keith's house and head out to the mine. The best part of the whole program was that we were home by 3 p.m. everyday unless we spent the night. We averaged between $700 and $900 every weekend.

We had no idea that the reason that gold and silver had skyrocketed was because a couple of gentlemen from Australia, the Hunt Brothers, were actually trying to corner the silver market by buying up all of the silver in the world. This was driving the price of gold and silver sky high.

Well, the party came to an end in the second week of December. The headlines in the paper said that the Hunt Brothers, in Australia, had been trying to corner the silver market. This drove the price of silver and gold up and when they were busted on the scam, the price of silver and gold started on a downward trend. We planned our last trip to the mine. There was still enough value to make it worth our while but gold was going down everyday, according to the newspaper.

We arrived at the mine that second Saturday in December and loaded the truck. Then we sat and barbequed burgers and drank cold beer. We spent the night at the mine and got up the next morning and we ate breakfast. After breakfast, I strolled around the mine and went over to the side shaft. Just then another truck pulled up to the mine. They were some of Keith's friends that worked at Southwest Kenworth.

It occurred to me that we had been coming to this mine for three months and nobody had rappelled down into the mine. I went back to the truck and pulled it up to the mine and tied a rope to the winch. Jim asked me," what in the world are you doing?" I told him I was going down into the mine. He laughed and then I started to lower myself down the side shaft. I went down about fifty feet and there was a landing at the first side shaft.

They were all up top and yelling down to me, asking me what was happening. I told them to send down a six- pack of beer because I was thirsty. They lowered down the beer. Then I heard Keith say that it could not be all that bad and that they were on their way down. I told them to bring a Coleman lantern and some flashlights because it was very dark. About ten minutes later, down came Keith and Jim and two of Keith's buddies. They let me walk in the lead.

I think we only went about thirty feet when I found a 30/40 Craig octagon barreled rifle and a wrench that was used to bend the track. I asked Jim why these items were still down here. He explained that in the old days, once the miners knew the mine was played out, they would walk away from the mines leaving all of their belongings behind. So I picked up the rifle and the wrench and took them with me.

We got over to the main shaft and started down the wooden stakes that were set up like a ladder. The wood like brand new. Jim said there was no moisture in the shaft, and as a result the wood didn't decay. We all had a rope on us just in case. About fifty feet further down in the main shaft we found a side shaft with a solid brass ore bucket. We hollered to the guys up top to bring up the ore bucket. We tied it to a rope and they pulled it to the surface.

About a hundred feet lower in the main shaft we found an ore car. Amazingly, the wheels were spinning. There was no way to explain why the wheels were spinning since there was no wind. We all spent the next twenty minutes getting that ore car to the surface. It was very heavy, and all we had was a rope to pull it up to the surface.

Jim and I proceeded to the bottom of the mine and found another side shaft. We went down the side shaft until it ended and then we saw a hole at the end that was about six inches in diameter. I flashed a light into the hole and sure enough there was a side shaft on the other side coming from another mine.

It looked like a room had been hollowed out and we could see a picnic table with playing cards on the table and several kerosene lamps. There were pistols and rifles lying around the room and we saw three Wells Fargo strong boxes. There was no way for us to blast because we did not have the rights to the mine. There was also some cash lying on the table. We looked at each other and headed to the surface.

Hoyt, Blu, Cal, Louise and Alec

Jim, Keith and I spent the next two months searching the area looking for the other mine. We had no luck. The surprising phenomenon was that once a shaft had been blasted over, time and the elements in the desert hide the shaft. A person can actually pass right by what was once the entrance to a mineshaft, and not know it exists. The desert is amazing. The whole terrain changes with rain and wind. We finally gave up looking for the mine. The price of gold had plummeted to $40 per ounce and the price of silver was down to $12 per ounce. At these prices it was not worth our while to continue collecting the ore.

I often thought about our adventure over the years and wondered what gang might have hung out in the bottom of that mine. None of us to my knowledge has ever been back to that mine and I am sure that it is still completely intact. I think we were a little scared thinking about how we had gone down in that mine, not knowing if there was air and we were very lucky that nobody had gotten hurt. We were not miners and we were not prepared for rappelling down into that mine. It was a spur of the moment situation, but a great adventure.

After our last trip, we packed up the trucks and I walked around the mine one last time. I noticed something under one of the yucca plants. I bent over and picked up what looked like a picture. It was a picture of three men and a lady sitting at a table. It looked they were having a great time. It looked like they were raising their glasses for a toast. I showed the picture to Keith. He laughed and said that they were probably visitors staying at Castle Hot Springs. He said that the background was definitely the resort. As we rode away from the mine I could not help but think that maybe they were folks that had hung out in the bottom of that mine. They had something to do with the history of that mine.

Chapter Two
Coming Home

The 1st World War had come to an end. It was November 1918. I was relieved to be done with fighting the war in France. I could see the Statue of Liberty in the distance from the deck of the ship as we approached Ellis Island. The battleship was bringing me, Alec Centro, and the rest of the military troops home from France. The ship was on its way to the naval base in New Jersey. I was so excited to be home. I had written my mother and father with the time of arrival and told them that I would be taking a train from New Jersey to New York City, my home.

All of my army buddies said goodbye to each other just before departing the ship. It was a chilly morning so they were all bundled up in their jackets. I overheard some of the guys complaining about the weather but I was just happy to be home. The weather in France was very similar to the weather in New Jersey, but at least I was home and not 5,000 miles away from this great USA. I hoped that I would see my friends again and we all agreed to stay in touch. In the back of my mind I knew that I would probably never see most of them again but I hung onto to the thought that we would not lose track of each other.

This whole war had been like a bad dream. I had spent two years in France. Some of my friends came back missing limbs and some did not make it at all. I could not understand why I made it back alive. Obviously by the grace of God I was home. I was very thankful to be alive. I waved goodbye to my friend Todd. He was headed home to Albany. Todd would be the nearest to me, just a four hour drive away.

Just before the end of the war, I spent more than three months in the infirmary in France, after having been exposed to mustard gas. I also started to experience a lot of pain in my knees, knuckles and other joints. It was always damp and cold in France. The climate was similar in New York. I knew that arthritis was in my family history and it was obvious that I had the symptoms of the disease.

I boarded the train to New York City, my home. The train arrived on time at Times Central Station and I could see a huge crowd waiting. I got off the train carrying my duffle bag. I looked around and tried to catch a glimpse of a familiar face in the crowd.

As I walked through the maze of people, I noticed a beautiful fair skinned girl with strawberry blonde hair blowing in the wind. As I approached her, my heart started to pound and I could feel my heart in my throat. It was Louise. She had come to meet me and I was surprised to say the least. I had kept a picture of her in my wallet these last two years, but just seeing her again made me begin to melt inside.

I could not believe how really beautiful she had become. The two of us had written each other over the past two years while I was serving in France. I had told her not to wait for me. I never dreamed that she would be there when I arrived.

Louise and I had grown up in the Bronx. My family ran a neighborhood butcher shop. I had worked in the butcher shop through my childhood and took pride in being a journeyman butcher. It was a trade passed on from two generations and I was glad to be part of the family business. Louise's father worked for the post office as the mail carrier in the neighborhood. Louise worked at a neighborhood dry cleaning establishment.

I reached for her and looked into her eyes. I held her in my arms, caressing her lovely face. I told her that I loved her and she told me that she loved me, and then we kissed. I could not believe the fire was still there after two years of being away from her. It appeared that our love had grown stronger even though we were apart. We left the train station and headed for Louise's apartment in our old neighborhood. She had a bottle of wine that was chilling in the icebox. We spent a good part of the evening making love and just enjoying each other's company.

I wanted to surprise my parents at the shop. I knew they would still be there even though it was late. When we entered the store my mother ran up and gave me a big hug. My father also hugged me and shook my hand. My parents expressed so much joy at seeing me home safe. They knew that I had been through a lot of medical issues this past year, while serving in France.

My mother then asked me when I was going to make an honest woman of Louise and marry her. I looked over at Louise and said, "Well, what do you think, Louise, will you marry me?" She told me that she had hoped for a more romantic setting for the proposal but she was not going to complain and said, "Yes, I would love to be your wife."

We left the butcher shop and went upstairs to the family flat for dinner. My mother had prepared my favorite meatloaf dinner. After dinner we headed back to the apartment to retire for the evening and discuss our wedding plans. Over-whelmed with emotion, I had to pinch myself to be sure that this was real. We were married one month from the day I arrived home from France.

I worked in the butcher shop as the head butcher. This gave relief to my father, who was suffering from arthritis. He helped out with the meat cutting and ran the shop. I worked for about two years but the pain in my joints just kept getting more severe. I finally went to a doctor who informed me that I, too, was suffering from arthritis. The doctor suggested that I consider moving to a hot dry climate such as Arizona. Another year went by. My pain continued to get worse.

Louise said she read about the climate in Arizona and that we should consider moving to Phoenix. She also read about a resort north of Phoenix that had natural hot sulfur springs right in the desert. The resort had cement spas and the water came out of the rocks and flowed from the highest pool and then continued down the mountain, flowing into several more man made spas and then out into Castle Creek. These springs supposedly had great healing powers for diseases like my arthritis.

It was called Castle Hot Springs and was a very upscale resort with rooms in the main hotel. She read there were also cottages that could be rented on the property. The food was rated as some of the best west of the Mississippi River. They also had a small golf course and tennis court on the grounds for the guests.

She said it was a very popular resort. She read that a lot of celebrities raved about the medicinal effects on their illnesses. She told me that she loved me very much and that we simply had to do something to help ease my pain. She also said that we had enough money set aside to go to the resort and stay for several months while we looked for work in nearby Phoenix. We talked about the move for another couple of months, but it was obvious to me that the move had become a necessity if Louise and I were to have any kind of life in the future.

Chapter Three
Heading to Phoenix

Louise and I boarded the train Monday morning in New York. Both of our families were there to see us off for the journey to Phoenix. It was very hard for my parents because it seemed like they just said goodbye to me when I left for the Army. It was a full five-day journey from New York to Phoenix.

The trip was absolutely beautiful. We traveled through the mid western part of the country. We were able to view all of the plains states from the train windows as we passed through the farming communities of our great country. The train was very comfortable and the food was outstanding. We were definitely tired of traveling when we finally arrived at the Phoenix railroad station right on schedule. Excited, we picked up our bags and got off the train.

We had the rest of our belongings sent to the San Carlos Hotel, which was only about three blocks north and eight blocks east of the train station. We boarded a cable trolley and it dropped us off right in front of the hotel. It was a beautiful eight-story hotel built with southwestern design. When we checked in, the man at the counter gave us a copy of the evening paper, the Phoenix Gazette. He said that they would deliver the morning paper right to our door every day.

Louise and I wanted to go to Castle Hot Springs as soon as possible, so I asked the front desk attendant how far it was. He said it was about fifty miles north of Phoenix. He said we could take the train to Wickenburg, but we needed to exit at Morristown. The resort had a stage bus that would meet us and take us to the resort about twenty miles northeast of Morristown. It was a regular run since the train arrived at Morristown every day at five o'clock in the evening to meet the resort's stage bus.

The attendant said we could also take the regular stagecoach that went to Wickenburg. He said it would drop us off in front of the resort right after the first way station at Bumble Bee. The stagecoach then went on its way to Crown King, which was a gold mining town and then continued on to Prescott. Castle Hot Springs was just a few miles west of Bumblebee. The way station was a place to stop and get a fresh team of horses and lunch.

The attendant said the stagecoach was a little cheaper than the train but it was an all day trip. He suggested that we take the train and the resort stage bus because it was a little safer and it would not kill the whole day. Also, I didn't want to breathe in all that dust from the stagecoach. We told him that we would decide in the morning.

We went up and settled into our room and then came down to the restaurant for dinner. I read the headlines and there had been several bank, train, and stagecoach robberies that had occurred over the past year and there were no leads on the identity of the bandits. No one had ever been hurt in any of the robberies according to the newspaper article. They usually struck late in the afternoon or early evening and then disappeared into the desert darkness leaving no trail. We had a lot of valuables and I was not sure that they would be safe on the stagecoach. We decided to take the desk attendant's suggestion, and took the train and the resort stage bus.

The next morning we had our bags taken back to the train station and headed to Wickenburg. It must have been the best route because when we got to the train station, there were three other couples that were also heading to the resort. They told us that the resort was a very popular location and was frequently visited by many celebrities. These people came from different parts of the country but we all had one thing in common, and that was the fact that we were all looking for a miracle.

The train arrived in Morristown right on time, at exactly five o'clock that evening. The resort stage bus, which was actually a large open-air bus, was already waiting. The resort employees loaded our luggage on the back of the bus. We all boarded immediately and sat in front of the luggage. The driver said that we had to leave immediately if we were to arrive before dinner.

We were about ten miles up the road north and east of Morristown when the driver stopped because of some large rocks that were in the road. The driver said that rockslides were a normal occurrence in the desert. He said that the rockslide may have been caused by a recent rainstorm.

We all got out for a minute to see if we needed to help him move the rocks. Suddenly, a bunch of masked men on horses came out from behind the bushes and declared, "Everybody put your hands high in the air!" We were in no position to argue with the five of them brandishing guns. One of them got off his horse and took all of our valuables including my grandfather's Rolex watch, which was engraved with his name, and my wedding ring.

The robbers took Louise's wedding ring and the diamond necklace that I had given her for our first wedding anniversary. They took all of the belongings from the other passengers and then fled into the twilight of the evening. We boarded the bus and were very distraught but glad nobody was hurt. We were very upset and the rough ride down that dirt road did not help matters. We traveled down the Castle Creek wash for the final five miles. It was a very desolate drive in pristine desert surroundings.

We could not find beauty in that drive, but as approached the resort, we found ourselves staring in complete amazement at what we saw. It was like an oasis. The property was about 12 acres, surrounded by mature palm trees. The huge front area was manicured rolling tiff grass with a little golf course molded in the center. We could see several of the hot spring pools, famous for their healing waters. We went by a tennis court in front of the main four-story hotel. Louise and I were full of anticipation about living at the resort.

We reported the robbery when we arrived. The deskman at the resort telegraphed the Maricopa County Sheriff, who was located in Phoenix, to let him know that the robbers had struck again. He also reported it to the Yavapai County Sheriff in Prescott. Castle Hot Springs is actually right near the border in Yavapai County, and though the robbery actually occurred in Maricopa County, both sheriffs were aware of the gang's operations. We were very upset because most of the items were not replaceable and had great sentimental value.

We checked into our room and Louise cried for an hour while I unloaded all of our belongings. We decided to go down to the spas and try to relax after our distasteful experience. The resort was quite crowded and we saw several actors from silent films. Ken Maynard, who was one of the first cowboy silent film actors, and Clark Gable were in one of the pools talking as we went looking for an available pool. There were a few politicians and several more actors and actresses enjoying the pools as well.

We entered one of the spas, which was the second to the last one on the property. We could smell the sulfur in the hot water. One of the guests, a gentleman, told us that we would get used to the heat and that we would both feel great. His name was Hoyt and he told us that he and his brother Cal were cattle ranchers. He told us that their ranch was about two miles east of the springs down the Castle Creek wash.

I asked him how they fed the cattle. He said that the cattle grazed in the desert. I was dumbfounded. I asked him what in the world do cows eat while grazing in the desert. I could not help but chuckle to myself. I was used to cattle grazing in large fields full of grass. He said that there were a lot of plants, grass and weeds, which made up most of their diet.

He was very knowledgeable and I asked him if there was ever water running down the wash. He said there was. In fact the reason there was such a build-up in front of the resort and the ranch was to divert the water when it rained. He pointed to the mountains and asked us to look closely. There simply is no place for the water to go. The rocks do not make good watershed, so all of the water from the mountains flows down to Castle Creek and that usually creates flash floods. He said they have seen walls of water as high as six feet running down the creek. It was hard to believe looking at the dry wash.

He was a very informative and pleasant fellow. We told him about the robbery and he ordered a drink for both of us. He apologized but stated that this was still very much the old west. We stayed in the pools for at least another two hours and visited with Hoyt and Cal. We had several more drinks with our new friends and headed off to bed. Louise and I made love with the moonlight shining in through the balcony window. I could not believe how good I felt. I was breathing fine and had no pain in any of my joints. We slept better that night than we had in years.

We saw our friends again the next morning during breakfast. They said that they had put in a long night of drinking. Hoyt said right after we retired for bed, they went to the other lounge to enjoy the live music. A country band played until closing time at 1 a.m. They invited us to join them on Saturday evenings.

Our friends told us that they would meet us at the spas at 7 o'clock and then we could join them again to party with the band at nine that night. We said we would love to join them. They said they had to leave to go back to their ranch to finish up branding the rest of the herd, but they would be back after dinner to join us. We said our goodbyes and headed down to the pools for some morning therapy.

As we sat in the pool and drank our juice, I looked through the classified section of the paper and tried to see if there was anything that looked promising in the area. There were a lot of opportunities, which really surprised me. One of the other guests told me that because of the dry hot climate, a lot of people were moving to Arizona for their health. His name was Max and he said that he was a pharmacist. He asked me what kind of work Louise and I did for a living. I told him that I was a butcher and he said, "How strange, I think the resort is looking to hire a butcher." I told him that Louise, my wife, worked at a hotel. He said that they could probably use both of us right here at the resort.

We were so excited that we went to our rooms and dried ourselves off and went right down to the desk to inquire about the job situation. The deskman told us that the manager would be back on Monday morning and that he would surely be interested. He said we should stop by again on Monday. He said that for the time being he would leave a message for the manager. He commented that it was very hard to find a journeyman butcher and they could really use someone with hotel experience. We were both very excited at the thought of being employed together here at the resort.

We picked up the morning paper and headed to the restaurant for a cup of coffee and to bring ourselves up to date with the news of the day. The front page of the newspaper was mostly dedicated to the robbery which we were victims to the day before. The Maricopa County Sheriff was asking for any information from the public that could help them solve these bizarre crimes. We were sure that we would not be recovering our stolen belongings.

Chapter Four
Enjoying the Resort

We spent the rest of that Saturday in the spa until three o'clock. We discussed the circumstances surrounding the robbery. We tried to sort through the details, so that we might be able to help the sheriff solve the crime. We went up to our room for a short nap. We were supposed to meet our new friends Hoyt and Cal for dinner that evening at six PM in the main resort restaurant. We had an evening of spirits and dancing planned. There was always live music on the weekends. We set our alarm for five PM so we would have time to get ready.

We woke before the alarm went off. We both jumped in the shower. We finished dressing and were ready to go in forty-five minutes. We left the room and headed to the restaurant. Saturday was always a barbeque. They specialized in Mesquite wood barbequed steaks and ribs. The steaks had a great taste due to the smoke and flame that rose from the Mesquite ambers. We had a wonderful dinner and drinks. Our new friends picked up the bill and insisted on paying the tab. We thanked them and then we all headed for the dance palace.

As we approached the dance hall we could hear the sounds of a banjo and fiddle. The musicians sounded like they had played together for a long time because they were really tight. It was only seven pm and the dance floor was full. We were surprised to see so many single women sitting at the bar and at the tables. We could not help but wonder where they all come from. Heck we were forty miles north of Phoenix and ten miles west of New River. I guess it did not matter because they were there and ready to party.

The resort was about twenty-five miles east of Wickenburg, which was actually the closest big town. The place was packed. We knew that all of these people were not staying at the resort. We just assumed that they were from the surrounding communities. We could see that Hoyt and Cal enjoyed the crowd. We all sat down at a table in the middle of the lounge and they ordered the first round of drinks.

Hoyt asked us where we had come from and how we heard about the resort. I told him that we were from New York. He laughed and said, "Boy, this place must be a huge change for you folks with the heat and the desert." We told him that we agreed completely but we thought that this part of the country was really beautiful. I told Hoyt that the area was just different than what we were used to but it had its own special beauty. I went on to tell him that I had been exposed to mustard gas in France during World War One. I told him that I had developed asthma and that the cold climate in New York made my arthritis pain almost unbearable. Louise thought Arizona would be the right ticket for me because of the hot dry climate.

I've always been so grateful, though, that my beautiful Louise was very healthy and had no physical problems. She read an article about Castle Hot Springs a year ago and it took that whole year to convince me to move out here and give it a try. Louise was willing to give p her family and friends in New York for the sake of my health.

Hoyt told us that he and Cal served in the US Calvary for ten years. Most of their career was spent chasing Pancho Villa. He told us that they were stationed in Columbus, New Mexico from 1915 to 1919. I told Hoyt that I had read a article in the New York Times about the Columbus, New Mexico. I believe the content of the story was about a raid by Pancho Villa. Hoyt and Cal were completely amazed at my knowledge about the raid. Hoyt asked me if I could remember the article.

I told Hoyt that there was an army post in the town and that the total population of the town was only 400. Villa's raiding party was 500 strong and was bigger than the town's total population. The article indicated that Villa raided the town in spite of President Wilson. Villa thought that Wilson was stirring up trouble between himself and his enemy, Vensustiano Carranza. Hoyt and Cal looked at us with a strange but comforting smile and Cal said, "Now we will tell you the real story."

"Hoyt and AI were in the 13th Calvary under Colonel Herb Slocum at the time of the raid. We can remember that day like it was just yesterday. It was March the 9th 1916 and it all started at 4:15AM. I was just getting off sentry duty and Hoyt was with me, because he was going to take my place for the next shift. Our garrison was about half full, about 100 men. Villa and his troops rode into town again about 500 strong, shooting in the air and yelling Viva Mexico. By the time we got the troops together to go out and confront them, Villa and his men had already robbed all of the stores in town of supplies and then took thirty to forty fine bred army mules and mounts."

"Make no mistake they were looking for food, supplies, ammunition, guns and mules. They thought the towns people would not put up a fight. We caught them by surprise, because they thought the garrison was empty. The shooting ensued and when it was over we had lost five troopers and Villa lost about twenty men. The whole conflict was over by 7 am that morning.

The good news was that we were able to capture one of Villa's colonels; his name was Colonel Vargas. He told us they were completely surprised that we had men at the post. He said they were informed that the garrison was almost empty. As it turned out the Colonel became a very good friend of ours and we are still good friends to this day.

We held him in our stockade for about a week and then orders came for us to escort him to Bisbee, for crimes against the surrounding border towns. Bisbee was the capital of the county and the warrants were issued from there. We were to proceed to Fort Huachuca after delivering him to the Sheriff in Bisbee. Our commander thought it would be best if just Hoyt and I escorted him so there would not be a lot of attention.

The ride took almost a week. It was a very long ride from Columbus to Bisbee, about three hundred miles. To pass the time we discussed many of the incidents. The Colonel went on to explain that they were waging war for the sake of freeing Mexico and only raided small towns in the southern Arizona and New Mexico area for supplies only.

Colonel Vargas went on to say that Villa was a good man and he explained that all of the stories about Pancho and his men murdering and raping women was all a bunch of bull. He said that Villa did not drink but he did loved women. The Colonel told us that Villa was an honorable man and a born leader.

Colonel Vargas went on to say, he had a very high position in the liberation army and that his enemies in Mexico City would love to get their hands on him. He told us that the US would deport him and then he would be shot when they got him to Mexico City. He told us that he was really wanted by his enemies. He told us that they would make an example of him. He asked us to let him go and if so that he and his country would be indebted to us for life.

Cal and I discussed the whole situation and we decided that it would be in the Colonel's best interest and that of Mexico to let him go. We had to make it look good or we would be in big trouble. We were about fifteen miles from Bisbee when we let him go. I shot Hoyt in the arm and the Colonel shot me in the thigh. We made sure that they were just superficial wounds and then we headed over to Fort Huachacha, which was only about 4 miles east of us for treatment of our wounds.

Colonel Vargas told us that he would get in touch with us at a later date to discuss a business plan that would take care of us for the rest of our lives. He told us that this was the least that he and his country could do for us for saving him from a fateful date with a firing squad. He told us that we were great men of foresight and wisdom.

We told him that talk was cheap but we believed in his cause and besides we might now qualify for disability and maybe even a discharge from the army with pay. We told him that we had grown very tired of the Army life. We also told him we were tired of chasing his boss Pancho Villa around the southwest. He laughed at us and then he waved and yelled audios Viva Mexico he then rode out of sight.

Cal and I rode on to the fort and went right to the post infirmary. The commander of the post came over to get our report. We told him that we were ambushed by a couple of Villa's men and during the shooting we both received wounds and we wounded one of Villa's men. The commander told us that he knew that Villa and his men were very illusive. He shook our hands and told us that he was happy that we came out of the incident alive.

I think we were in the hospital for about a week and then the commander ordered us back to Columbus to proceed with our discharge. It took us a week to get back to Columbus. We were still in pain from our wounds so the riding went slower than usual. We were there about a month for our disability to be approved but the day came and we received our papers and said goodbye to all of our friends. We received full retirement pay because we were injured on the job. We headed home to our ranch and our folks were very happy to see us when we arrived two weeks later.

Hoyt said, "Well that is enough of that, now let's have some fun." We spent the evening dancing and drinking and thoroughly enjoyed our new friends. They both seemed to know all of the people there so we figured they were regulars. Louise and I were pretty tipsy by the end of the evening. The food, drink and dancing had taken its toll. We had a great time with our new companions but Louise and I decided to call it a night. We said goodbye and we headed to our room. Louise was still a little tipsy so my mind started to wander. I hoped that the evening might end with a love encounter.

I just could not believe how good I felt especially after a long evening of dancing and socializing. I would normally be shot if I was back in New York. I still had a ton of energy. This place truly had healing waters and the dry heat was also great for my arthritis. The air was so clean and clear that my lungs felt great. My lungs were so clear.

During the walk back to our room, I pointed to the sky and showed Louise the Big Dipper. Louise said that she could not remember it being this clear in New York. She said she thought the sky was the clearest that she had ever seen. She told me that she was very happy that they had come out here. She said she missed our families but this was definitely now our home. We arrived at our room and undressed and got ready to go to bed for the night.

We looked over at the dresser and sure enough there sitting on the dresser was her wedding ring, diamond necklace and my grandfathers Rolex watch. We both looked at each other in total amazement. We could not figure out what happened. We finally deducted that the robbers must have left them for us. There was a little note on our dresser. "We cannot keep valuables that belong to our friends." The note was signed, "The Ghost Riders."

We went to bed and hugged each other. We laid there on the bed for quite a while discussing the situation. We finally realized that somehow our paths crossed with the Ghost Riders. We had met so many new friends that we could not figure out who they were. They could be anyone of a dozen new friends. The minute our heads hit the pillow we were asleep. It had been a long day with a lot of excitement, to say the least.

The next morning we rose from bed. We were still excited about the return of our belongings. We got dressed and headed down for breakfast. Hoyt and Cal were there and had already ordered their breakfast. They asked us to join them and they proceeded to tell us that they were too damn drunk to ride home so they stayed overnight at the resort. In talking with them we deducted that this was a pretty regular occurrence on the weekends for the boys. They told us that they worked very hard all week and that the weekends were for relaxation.

They told us that they would be away for about ten days. They said they had to go to Prescott on cattle business. They told us that they would have to stop off at Crown King on the way back for other business. Crown King was the next way station on the way to Prescott. They told us that it was a small mining community. They told us that the main mine was the Orabelle mine but that the area was filled with gold mines in the vicinity. They told us that the town had one bar, a restaurant, general store with a post office and one hotel.

They told us that the ore was taken by buckboard from the mine, which was about six miles down the road to Crown King. The ore was then transported by rail down the mountain to Cleator. Cleator is the official assay office. The ore is weighed, processed and estimated for the government. The army then paid the mine and they then were responsible for transporting the gold to Phoenix and then on to the Denver Mint.

Later that morning the Sheriff and one of his deputies arrived at the resort. The deskman sent over one of hotel employees so that we could meet with him and his deputy to go over the facts about the robbery. We went with him across the property to the main building. When we entered the building there sitting in the lobby were two men that just looked like lawmen. They had cowboy hats on with boots and both had guns strapped on their hips. They both rose from their chairs and extended their hands in friendship. The sheriff was William Perry and his deputy's name was Lance Alder. They were very nice and started the conversation by apologizing for the robbery.

The Sheriff asked most of the questions. The deputy just listened, very intently I might add. We told him the whole story. We did leave out the fact that the robbers had returned our stolen items. We felt a little uncomfortable divulging information about the robbery. We knew that sooner or later they would come forward. It was a very awkward situation.

This was the first time in our lives that we withheld information from the law but it just seemed to be the right thing to do. We both knew we were wrong but neither of us could muster the guts to say anything. The sheriff told us that they had no leads and that they could not figure out how the gang was fencing the stolen merchandise. Usually the stolen items would show up in circulation but not with this gang. He said the gang normally struck just before dark and then would disappear into the dark of the desert. He told us that they had been in business for a little over three years. He said they were no closer now than when they were three years ago. We could tell that the sheriff was very discouraged. They left us a business card and told us to contact them if we thought of any details not mentioned.

We relaxed the rest of that Sunday in anticipation of the possibility of work the next day. We were low on funds and needed work soon. We strolled around the resort and talked about the return of our stolen belongings. They meant so much to us. They were all very personal items. We wondered who these Ghost Riders were. We knew that we had met them. It was all very exciting business.

Chapter Five
Finding a Way of Life

The alarm went off and it was Monday morning. We both woke up and each of us took a shower. We got dressed and headed for breakfast. It was about 9 a.m. when we finished our breakfast. Then we strolled over to the front desk and asked if we could see the manager. The front desk clerk answered the phone and mentioned to us that the manager would be right out to meet the two of us.

A door opened from behind the desk and a tall gentleman with a handlebar mustache came over to us, extended his hand and introduced himself as Jim Stanhouse. He mentioned that he heard that we were both looking for work. He knew that I was a butcher. He asked me if I would consider working part time since there was not enough business to keep someone on in that capacity on a fulltime basis.

He said that they would keep me busy the rest of the time helping out around the kitchen or working maintenance. He told Louise that they needed a concierge and explained the job to her. We were both very excited and after he went over the wages, we were sold. He asked us when we could start and we said immediately. He said "How about next Monday?" We told him that would be perfect.

One of the benefits was a free room in one of the two Victorian homes on the property. One of the homes was a guesthouse, and the other house was occupied by the manager. There was a room upstairs that would be ours. We also had free use of all of the resort's amenities. We both felt this was a great start, at least until we knew what direction we wanted to go for our future.

We both knew for sure that we loved it out here in Arizona. We both loved the resort and were very happy, especially since we had our belongings back. We just wondered about our new friends. The whole situation was very exciting. We enjoyed the resort and all of its amenities for the balance of the week and then right after dinner on Friday we headed to the lounge. There were Hoyt and Cal back from their trip, sitting at a table. We were very glad to see them.

They asked us to join them at their table and said that they had a lot to tell us about the past week. They both extended their hands and shook my hand and then gave Louise a hug. It was amazing how we had become such good friends in such a short time. I ordered us all a drink and Hoyt asked us how the week went. We told him that we enjoyed the resort and that it had been very relaxing.

We told him that on Monday we both hiked down the wash and went by their ranch. We saw several ranches along the wash and they all were built up in front to divert the water during flash floods. They told us that most of the time the wash was dry, until we would have a heavy rainstorm. He told us that their family had lived there for over fifty years. He said the ranching business was a tough way to make a living especially right now for the past couple of years. The price of beef had been on a downhill slide. They had to find other work to make ends meet. We really did not want to pry into their affairs so we left it at that.

We told him that on Wednesday we hiked north and west and after about two miles we discovered an abandoned mine. We told them that it looked like it had been a very successful mine at one time. We wondered how long it had been abandoned. We found old bottles at a building that looked like it was some type of bar but it was now being used as a stable. There was a herd of wild horses grazing around the mine. They told us it was the Copperopolis gold mine.

They said that gold had been discovered in 1893 and that the mine even had a general store and bar. We asked him where the miners lived and Hoyt told us that they simply pitched tents around and lived in them. He went on to say that the life of a miner was rough and lonely. It got very hot and miserable during the summer months because they did not have any means of cooling. Their only salvation was actually during work hours because down in the mine it is about sixty-five degrees all year round.

The other good thing about Copperopolis was that it was only two miles from Castle Hot Springs. He said that the miners did spend quite a bit of time at the resort. He said the mine was played out in 1915 and that it had been abandoned since then. He told us that had been one of the largest gold strikes in Arizona.

We could see there was a mountain of quartz about one hundred yards south of the mine. He explained to us that the quartz was simply the left over ore after the gold and silver had been removed. He told us that a couple of miners discovered a vein of gold on the surface and then they just followed the vein down into the ground.

No telling what direction they would go, but they blasted and a shaft was formed. He said that they would bring the ore to the surface in an ore bucket and then the ore was transported to the crushing plant on the site. They would always have a side shaft to be used for escape in case of a cave-in. Several other shafts led from the main shaft to the side shaft at different levels to be used for exits.

It sounded like a hard job. He said that mining was definitely hard work. They also built the rail systems. The rail had ore cars that were used to carry the loads of ore to the main shaft. From there the ore was hoisted to the surface in ore buckets. Inside the main shaft was a large pipe about six inches in diameter that went all the way from the top of the mine to the bottom. Hoyt told us that this pipe was used to pump air into the mine. He said there was usually a windmill at the surface. There was a lot of area in the side shafts that did not have air so the miners would have to pump air to the bottom so there would be plenty of oxygen for them to breathe the next day.

We finished the first round of drinks and Louise ordered a second round. We were drinking the second round when Hoyt mentioned that they were going to catch the train in Morristown on Tuesday. They were headed out to meet their friend Colonel Vargas on business in Tucson. They asked us if we wanted to accompany them. They said that they would be gone for just about a week. They told us that it would be a chance for us to see more of this new state.

We were kind of excited but we told them that we were ready to start our new jobs and that we would have to pass for right now. We told him that we were almost broke and that we needed the jobs. Hoyt said, "That's okay. We get together every month, so there will be another time." We left it at that and said he said they would let us know the next time.

As we sat together at the table one of the waiters took our picture. We all raised our glasses and Hoyt proposed a toast, "Let us all live long productive lives and prosper at all our endeavors!" We spent the rest of the evening enjoying the music, drink and friends. We both looked forward to the following Monday. We were going to start our new jobs and our new life at the resort.

We were definitely going to miss our new friends but we knew that they would return in a couple of weeks. We said good night at closing time. Hoyt said that when they returned that he and Cal would bring over a couple of horses and take us back to the mine to show us around the area. We were thrilled. These guys were a lot of fun and they had tremendous knowledge of the territory. We all got up and shook each other's hands. They said that they would see us soon.

As we finished our drinks Louise looked over at me and said "Alec, did you figure out yet who the Ghost Riders are? " I said, "Not really." She said, "It is pretty obvious that it is Hoyt and his brother Cal." I looked at her after thinking it over for a while and said, "You are right." "Why didn't I figure that out!" She said that we had become such good friends and it was hard to believe they could be the thieves. We would have to confront them when they returned.

Probably our best opportunity would be when they were to take us for the horseback ride. We would be away from everybody and alone so that no one could overhear our conversation. Louise said that she thought that they wanted to share their story with us but they needed us to make the first move. I said, "Well, great because I can't wait to talk to them when they return."

Chapter Six
The Proposal

We spent the next day, Sunday, relaxing around the resort. We truly enjoyed the waters of the hot pools. We could not stop talking about Hoyt and Cal. Now that we figured out whom, they were, our minds were going a thousand miles an hour. Why were they robbers was the big question in both of our minds. We were very cautious when talking about them. Louise said that there must be a lot more involved than meets the eye. These two were just too smart to be normal thieves.

She said that she thought that this Colonel they were seeing had something to do with their situation. She also felt that the mine came into play in some way. We were anticipating their return and hoped that they would get home safe and be able to share more about themselves. Louise mentioned that one interesting fact was that in all of the robberies that no one had ever been shot. They apparently were smart thieves but they were not killers. These guys were definitely "Ghost Riders."

We both agreed that it was a very exciting situation. We made sure that we read the paper every morning. We also had the deskman dig up all of the old papers that he could find. We hoped these old papers would help us understand more about the Ghost Riders. The robbers did their homework and had a pretty good idea about the take on each job. They left no clues or tracks, but we guessed that they learned a lot after spending a good part of ten years in the cavalry. They also knew the general area and the terrain, which gave them a huge advantage.

We had dinner that night and focused our attention on the following Monday, anticipating the start of our new jobs. It could not have come at a better time. We just had ten dollars to our name. We moved all of our belongings into our room in one of the Victorian houses on the property. We enjoyed another dip into the miracle waters of the spas and then enjoyed a delicious dinner while watching the most beautiful sunset.

This was the best evening we'd experienced at the resort. We took a little walk around after dinner and headed to our room. We both anticipated the next day and our new jobs. But in the back of our minds we could not get Hoyt and Cal out of our thoughts. We hoped the best for our new friends.

We went to bed early that night and woke early the next morning. We went to the kitchen and had a marvelous breakfast. Then we both walked across the property to the resort and started the training for our new positions. When we broke for lunch we picked up the evening paper and there was an article on the front page about the "Ghost Riders." We both chuckled to ourselves. There were still no clues that could bring an end to the robberies. The week went on and we both enjoyed learning about our new jobs.

Living at the resort was just what the doctor ordered. The week ended and we spent the time off relaxing around the resort. We did not go to the lounges that weekend because we were broke. We were paid on a bi-weekly basis, so we wouldn't be able to celebrate until the next weekend. The following week went by with no real incidents other than me hurting my back while lifting a side of beef. I took some aspirin Tuesday and Wednesday nights and by Thursday I was fine.

We both were getting off work Thursday night and as we walked by the lounge, we heard a shout from the lounge. Somebody was calling my name. We both peeked in the door and there were Hoyt and Cal. They invited us in to have a drink and share some conversation. They said they had a lot to tell us.

Hoyt asked if we would be ready to go for the ride that they promised us before they left. We told them that we would be ready by the weekend. They said they would be by with the horses after breakfast on Saturday morning about 8 a.m. We told them we would be ready. They told us to wear jeans and dress warm because it is still a little cold in the desert in the fall of the year. We finished our drink and said goodnight to our friends. We shook hands and said we were glad that they had come back safely.

We went to bed early again that evening. We were both tired but it had been great to see our friends. We rose the next morning and started off to work. The day went by fast, as did all of the days. The work was not hard but it kept us busy. We went by the manager's desk and received our pay for the past two weeks. The timing could not have been better, because we were totally broke. We celebrated by going out for dinner and sure enough Hoyt and Cal were also there so we sat with them.

After dinner we all went over to the lounge and enjoyed an evening of drinking and dancing. We finished a couple of rounds of drinks, and about 9 p.m. we got up and told them we had to go to bed early if we were still on for the ride in the morning. Hoyt said that they would be by the next morning to pick us up. He told us to be ready at 8 o'clock.

We said goodnight and strolled across the property to our room. Before we went to sleep, Louise suggested that we let the day dictate the right time. She said that we would know when to discuss our findings with them. We were asleep the minute our heads hit the pillows.

We woke the next morning with great anticipation about the day. We ate our breakfast in the house. Cindy, the chef, had breakfast every morning at 7 a.m. in the kitchen. This was one of the benefits of our job. Our room and board and two meals a day were part of the payment for working at the resort. There were about six other couples that also had this setup for employment at the resort.

We walked across the property to the gate and at about two minutes after eight, Hoyt and Cal rode up to where we were waiting. Each of them had an extra horse saddled and ready to go. We explained to them as we mounted our horses, we had not been horseback riding for a couple of years. They said that it would be okay because the horses do all of the work and that we would not be riding fast. We just needed to make sure that we hung on and didn't fall. The rocks are not very forgiving and usually the fall results in serious injury. We told him that we were decent riders and that we should be able to stay on the horses.

We left from the east side of the property and headed northeast down Castle Creek. I think that we rode about three miles. Hoyt and I rode next to each other in the lead. Louise and Cal rode next to each other behind Hoyt and me. We started to slow down a little and I saw Hoyt looking around. We then turned north and headed up a trail. We went up a hill that was a pretty steep incline. We finally arrived at the top of the hill.

The view was breathtaking. We started down the hill on the other side into a wash heading northwest. It was hard for me to tell, but it looked like we were on a trail. We proceeded down that wash and then we went up another mountain. Continuing northwest, we headed back down into yet another wash. I would have been lost for sure, but Hoyt certainly knew his way to wherever we were going. The next mountain was quite a bit higher but I could see the trail. We rode about another two miles and then Hoyt headed due east down another wash and up the next mountain.

When we reached the top I could see the tower over the mine in the distance. It was about a quarter of a mile from us. I pointed it out to Louise. We were both amazed because it was the same mine that we had discovered in our hike earlier in the week. We simply had arrived from a different direction. We rode over to the main shaft, which was about a hundred feet from the side shaft. We told Hoyt and Cal this was the mine that we had discovered while out riding, the one that we all had discussed earlier before they left for Mexico.

He pointed to an old building that he said was a bar originally but now had been converted into a stable. Hoyt said, "I wish we could stop here so I could explain the operation a little more, but we have to ride just a little further to reach our destination." We continued on west of the mine and down the hill about two hundred feet below the big mine, which Hoyt said was the Copperopolis Mine.

When we reached the bottom we were in another wash. We rode a little north and east about a hundred feet in the wash and then Hoyt and Cal dismounted their horses. They asked us to dismount. Hoyt told us to follow him single file. We began walking back southeast of the wash and sure enough a cave opened up in the rocks. There was no way that anyone could have seen the cave unless they knew exactly where it was located. You could ride up and down the wash and never know it was there. Hoyt told us that it was a mine. He said that Colonel Vargas told him that Pancho Villa used the mine as a hideout.

He said that the miners discovered a vein of gold and it went straight into the mountain about two hundred feet and then the vein ended and they just left and the one shaft is all that exists. The old miners set up a pull line and hauled the ore up the mountain to the crushing plant. He explained that was the reason there was no shale lying around the mine. It was a perfect hideout. There were no traces that it even existed. The wood posts had been removed, but you could still see pieces of the posts that were in the ground. Pancho

Villa and his men had removed the wood and the pull line to help conceal the mine.

Hoyt lit a kerosene lamp and led the way into the mine. We went back about two hundred feet and just before the mine ended there was a large room that had been built by the miners or perhaps Pancho Villa's gang. The mine shaft itself was very large, about eight feet wide and ten feet high. The room at the end was at about twenty-five feet long and fifteen feet high. We tied the horses to a hitching post at the entrance of the large room. It actually was a little cool in the mine.

Cal told us that the temperature was about sixty degrees all year round. I noticed a hole about eight inches in diameter at the end of the room. Cal told us that the miners ran into a side shaft from the Copperopolis mine. He said that was how they knew that it was no use going any further. I mentioned to him that it was obviously rare that they could have run into another shaft from another mine. Hoyt said, "Yes, about a million to one."

He lifted the lantern next to the hole and we could see the other shaft. He gave each of us a lantern and told us that the light would help if we had claustrophobia. We found out very quickly that neither of us did. It was very bright with all four lanterns lit. In the middle of the room was a picnic table with a deck of cards on the table. We also saw money and guns sitting on the table. There were several beds set up next to the walls of the shaft and a couple of Wells Fargo strong boxes stacked up next to the beds.

Louise looked over at me and exclaimed, "Alec, I told you the mine had something to do with them." I said, "Louise, you were right." Cal told us that they wanted to show us the mine because they felt comfortable with us and they had a proposition for us. I told them Louise and I had a million questions running through our minds. We sat down at the table and Hoyt passed us a canteen. We all took a swig of water. It really tasted good.

Hoyt started by telling us that when they arrived back at the ranch from being released from the cavalry, they found out from their folks that the money they had been sending home was just enough to sustain them. Their parents said most of the cattle had been rustled and all they had were the chickens and hogs. Their parents said they tried to make a go of the ranch but with the rustlers and the dropping meat prices, they were going broke.

Hoyt told us that he and Cal stayed on at the ranch and tried to make a go of it. They were doing okay after about a year of hard work. About then, they received a wire from Colonel Vargas. He asked them to meet him in Nogales to discuss the potential business proposition that he offered just before "escaping" from them on the way to Bisbee. Hoyt told us that he and Cal boarded the train at Morristown and headed for Phoenix.

They continued through Phoenix and on to Tucson. Then they rode their horses from Tucson to Nogales. The Mexican train begins in Nogales and heads south to Mazatlan. Hoyt told us that he and Cal arrived in Nogales just in time for dinner. Colonel Vargas and several of his men met them at the border crossing.

They all shook hands and then headed to a local restaurant for dinner. Hoyt said that the dinner was great and they spent the rest of the evening drinking and visiting with their friend Colonel Vargas. They told us that they needed to get reacquainted because it had been a couple of years since they had seen each other.

Holt leaned back and told us the story. "Colonel Vargas said that life had been good but that Mexico was going through another independence battle. He said that the heroes of the war had been rewarded with land in Mexico. He told us that he had put a piece of property in our name as a reward for helping him escape."

"We were completely taken by surprise. He told us there was a piece of property in each of our names and that he had wanted us to see our land. He said he had purchased train tickets for us and that we were headed to Mazatlan in the morning so he could show us our land. He wanted us to see what a great life that we could have living in Mexico. He said that the train was leaving at 9 p.m. and that it took all night to get to Mazatlan via train."

"We finished dinner and visiting and walked across the street to the train station. The Colonel's men had already loaded all of our horses on the train and we boarded with Colonel Vargas. We were in the last train car. It was going to be an interesting ride. People had dogs, cats, hogs and one lady had billy goat. Colonel Vargas smiled and said they had a very easy life style here in Mexico. He went on to say that Mazatlan was over five hundred miles south of Nogales but we would be sleeping most all of the way."

"Colonel Vargas told us that Mazatlan was in Jalisco County which was semi-tropical. He told us we would be there just after dawn the next morning. Actually, the train ride was not all that bad. With the constant rolling of the train tracks, we slept like babies. We arrived in Mazatlan just after dawn just as Colonel Vargas had promised. We disembarked the train and a troop of the Colonel's soldiers met us. We boarded a carriage and headed to the boat docks. The Colonel said we needed to hurry because breakfast was waiting at our new home."

"We left the train station and arrived at the boat dock about twenty minutes later, just after the sun had risen. The view of the Pacific Ocean was spectacular. In the distance I could see an island. As I gazed out into the ocean, I thought I saw a whale blowing. Colonel Vargas told me that I was right.

The island is a whaling village during the whaling season. Then, the rest of the year it serves as a fishing port. We all boarded what looked like a fishing boat. Colonel Vargas's men loaded our baggage on to the boat and told us that the horses, would be stabled until we left."

Hoyt stretched his leg, and then continued on with his story. "I think we went about eight miles and then we went on by the island we had seen from the mainland. The Colonel pointed to another island on the opposite side of the fishing port. It was a beautiful place with a lot of greenery and one big mountain in the middle. He said this island was our destination. We arrived about fifteen minutes later and docked the ship. We all exited the ship and climbed onto the buckboards. Then the Colonel headed toward the top of the hill."

"The road wound around and in between a lot of thick trees and plants. The Colonel said that the shrubs were banana trees and rubber plants. He told us that the plants were all native to the island. We arrived at the top and the mountain was actually a large plateau with a plantation. We could see a beautiful large ranch house. We went through the courtyard. Two large double doors opened into another entry area inside the home. The floor of the home was saltillo tile. It had a beautiful finish. Colonel Vargas explained that the finish was important because the tile was very porous and the varnish protected the tile from getting stains."

"The living room was to the left with the dining area behind it. We walked by the living room and dining room to the back where the kitchen was situated and the Colonel led us right by the kitchen and dining area to a large patio that overlooked the Pacific Ocean, which lie below us. The view was spectacular."

"There were folks everywhere working. The Colonel said that breakfast would be served on the patio. He led us back into the home and along the left of the hall were five bedrooms. The home had one indoor bathroom and one outhouse. All of the rooms in the home were furnished with Mexican style leather and bamboo furniture. We went back out on the patio and a servant brought us a glass of wine. The Colonel smiled, and rose from his chair and with the wine in one hand he waved his other arm around and asked us what we thought of the place. Cal and I told him that it was heaven."

"Colonel Vargas smiled and said that the home and island belonged to us. We were so shocked that we did not know what to say. We thought the place belonged to him. We were astounded. Our heads were swimming. We both got up out of our chairs and approached the Colonel. We could hear the waves crashing against the rocks below. We could see a trail from the back of the patio down to the ocean, which was about one hundred feet below us. We could also see about a quarter of a mile to the east that there was a beautiful beach."

"The Colonel smiled again, and then asked if we liked this home. We told him that we were without words. Simply put, this was as good as it gets. We asked him how this was possible. He explained that heroes of his country are treated like kings. We both saved him and the new president was extremely thankful. He reached into his pocket and handed us the deed to the property. He went on to tell us that the maid, the cook, and the caretaker were also part of the gift. He introduced Jose, Maria and Pablo. He told us that they lived on the property in their own quarters."

"The Colonel went on to tell us that the property that was deeded to us was about five acres. He told us that the five thousand dollars that we each had invested would be enough to pay for the servant's wages. He said that we should be set for life. All we needed was to come up with another ten thousand dollars and with their economy for sure we would be set. The whole situation just seemed to be unreal. Colonel Vargas then invited us to sit down on the patio with him. He ordered another round of wine for all of us. He told us that he was ready to answer any questions."

Hoyt shifted in his seat, and continued. "I looked over at Colonel Vargas and again thanked him and then went on to say that Cal and I would have to do something to keep the place afloat. We were just cattlemen and like fish out of water down in Mexico. Colonel Vargas invited us to walk down to the beach with him. He told both of us that he had a fool proof program worked out if we were willing to give the idea a whirl."

"As we walked along the beach a beautiful young girl came past us. She smiled, and Cal and I looked at each other. We could read each other's minds. We definitely had to find a way to live here. The Colonel must have noticed us smiling at the girl. I looked at him and smiled and said that I have two eyes and I can dream. He said that this section of the beach was part of our property. He said that the section that belonged with the property was about a quarter of a mile long. He smiled and then invited us back up to the patio so he could explain the plan that he had devised that would allow us to move into the property permanently in a couple of years."

"Colonel Vargas suggested that we become robbers and that he would fence all of the stolen property and money in Mexico. He said that since the loot would not be surfacing in the United States that it would be impossible for the authorities of the US to trace the goods. He said that by disposing of the goods that it would help his country and keep the law from finding us. He said it would be a daring business, and even though he would help minimize the risk of being caught, it was still risky business."

"He told us that he would meet us in Tucson about every six weeks to pick up the loot. The Colonel made arrangements with several folks to create a chain of fences to dispose of the stolen property. He said that he would invest the money in the government bonds. He figured that with a little luck that it would only take a couple of years to get enough funds to set us up for the rest of our lives in Mexico."

"Cal and I were both excited about the proposition, and we both agreed that we could be robbers but not killers. We told the Colonel that we would die first before shooting anyone during a robbery. He told us that he understood, and that if we thought out our robberies that we could keep the chances of that happening to a minimum."

"Colonel Vargas suggested that we keep the stolen merchandise in the mine as it was a perfect place to store the goods until they could be transported. He said that it was next to impossible to track in the desert. The mine was close enough to the ranch and the resort at Castle Hot Springs. Our odds would be better if we were careful and planned our robberies. The main idea was to not get greedy. We simply needed to take what was available and then move on to the next job. We figured that we could not pull the jobs by ourselves and that we would need a third partner."

Louise looked at Hoyt and asked, "What about the third man? Who is he?" Hoyt smiled and said, "Well you don't miss much. We will be meeting the third man later." We respected his position.

Hoyt continued, "Later, we headed back across the water from the island to Mazatlan. We boarded the train and headed back to Nogales and then on to Morristown. We just came back from our latest meeting with Colonel Vargas. We were there for the past two weeks. We went all of the way down to Mazatlan so that we could get a glimpse at paradise to help us continue our quest."

Louise and I were listening intently, but we were really getting thirsty. Hoyt passed us the canteen and we both took a drink. Cal then reached over and grabbed a bottle of Jack Daniels Whiskey. He took a swig, passed it to Hoyt, who took a swig and then he passed it to both Louise and myself and we also took a drink. Hoyt then poured us all a shot and he offered a toast to our health and future. We all downed the shot.

Louise spoke. She got right to the point. She asked Hoyt why they told us the story. Hoyt told us that he and Cal were very impressed with our knowledge of the West, and they enjoyed our company, but most of all they had a proposition for us. They felt that we might be folks looking for a little adventure and excitement in our lives. Louise and I smiled and then I spoke up and told them, "Well, guys you have us pegged right on the money from one stand point. We are looking for excitement that is for sure but we do not want any part of robberies."

Hoyt went on to say that they had no intentions of getting us involved in robberies. They could not take a chance on novices at this point. He said that they had the robbery business down to a science. They had one glitch in their network of people that helped them fence the goods. He said that Colonel Vargas was about to retire and they needed someone to take his place in fencing the stolen merchandise in Mexico.

Hoyt said that they needed somebody that they could trust. He and Cal felt that if they make us partners in the business that we would be straight with them. They also needed to have someone take care of their home on the island outside of Mazatlan.

They had spoken with Colonel Vargas about their plan and he was willing to set us up with all of the contacts in the underground network. Also, the law was getting close to their operation and they needed new faces involved to throw the law off their trail. As payment for helping them, they were willing to set us up in our own home on the island and that they had amassed enough money for all of us. They only needed a couple more jobs to be set financially for the rest of their lives. We told Hoyt and Cal that we would think about the proposal.

We told him that we were both very excited about the offer. Hoyt told us that the weather was quite similar to the Arizona climate. He did say that we would be near the ocean and that he was not sure if the dampness would affect my asthma and arthritis. He told us that the weather stayed pretty much the same almost all year long.

We finished our shots of Jack Daniels and headed out. As we rode away from the mine I turned to Hoyt and told him that we would need to know the third person if we were going to commit. He said that would be fine once we made a decision. He said that for now they wanted to leave him out of the picture to protect his identity.

We finally arrived back at the resort. By now it was lunchtime. The morning had gone by so fast we could not believe it was already noon. We told them that we were famished and that we would meet them for dinner and by then we would make our decision. We told them that we were excited and that it was a great offer. We told them that we had a lot of thinking to do to get the whole situation straight in our minds. We thanked them for sharing everything with us and told them no matter what that we could be trusted.

Chapter Seven
The Decision of Our Lives

Louise and I assured Hoyt and Cal that we would have an answer by the time we were to meet them for dinner that evening at the barbeque. We said goodbye and then headed for our room. We did not speak on the walk. We had just settled into our room, which was pretty spacious. It had a rocking chair and a second story balcony.

We stepped onto the balcony and we could see Hoyt and Cal leaving. We held each other closely, hugging but not saying one word to each other. They glanced over at the house and when they saw us on the balcony they waved to us. We really liked both of them and they definitely did not hold back telling us what they were thinking. We liked this western attitude. The attitudes back east were totally different. The truth of the matter was that we had only read about men like Hoyt and Cal but what a thrill it was to have met them and really know them. I think it was about an hour later before one of us said a word.

Louise looked at me and said, "I think that if we are to consider this that we need to see the property in Mexico and take that trip the next time that the guys leave to meet Colonel Vargas." She went on to say, "If we can see our future home and experience a little bit of the way of life. It would make it easier to make our decision." She asked what I thought. I told her that I could not agree more.

We both laid down on the bed to take a nap. We could not sleep because our heads were really swimming deep in thought. We could not fall asleep. We had too much on our minds. We discussed the possibilities and both of us got very excited. We were ready to give the brothers our answer or at least what we were thinking about the whole situation. Louise told me that she thought that I should do the talking because we both knew what we wanted.

We got up out of the bed at about 4 p.m. and we both took a shower. Our emotions got the best of us during the shower. We went back to bed and made passionate love. We stayed in the bed until around 5 o'clock. We both got up and got dressed and I sat on the balcony while Louise got herself ready. We headed over to the barbeque at about a quarter to six.

Hoyt and Cal were already sitting at their regular table. We said hello and they asked us to join them. We ordered a drink and sat down. We could smell the steaks cooking, and they smelled great. We were all very hungry. Hoyt, not wasting anytime, asked me if we had made a decision. I asked him to step outside and take a walk. I told him that Louise and I had discussed the situation at great lengths.

We agreed that we wanted to go with them on their next trip to Mexico to meet Colonel Vargas and the rest of the people in the chain. We told him that we also wanted to see this home in Mazatlan, Mexico. I told him that we were both excited about going with them on their next trip. We decided it would only be right to experience the whole program before making a definite decision.

I did not know what to expect from Hoyt. He laughed and said, "It sounds great to me, and we both will go along with your wishes." I told him that we would have to get permission from the resort. The manager told us that if we were only gone a week, it would not be a problem. Hoyt said that we would definitely enjoy the trip and everybody would be happy to meet us.

Hoyt told us that it would be a few months until they would be ready again. He said they had a lot of work to do and would have to be very careful. He had a feeling that the law was probably getting close to catching them. Hoyt and

Cal left that night, and we did not see the two of them for at least a month.

There was no report of any robberies for almost three weeks and then the paper reported that the Ghost riders hit the train going to Tucson just north of Casa Grande. The paper reported that there was a newly formed group of lawmen called the Arizona Rangers. A few of them were on board the train during the robbery and the leader swore to the reporter that he was going to find the perpetrators. The paper said that the gang got away with over $5,000 in cash and $3,000 in jewelry.

The Arizona Ranger told the reporter that the gang left several clues, and that he would follow up on all clues and any information that the public could provide. He had gotten off the train at Casa Grande. He rounded up four more rangers. They then returned to the scene of the robbery. They started tracking the gang north toward Phoenix. We were very concerned for our friends, but truthfully, they were robbers and criminals, and that is a very dangerous business.

Louise thought that it was very strange that the Ghost Riders were out of the area that they normally worked. She looked over and asked me if I thought they were in Mexico again. I told her that Hoyt would have let us know if they were going to Mexico. She said, "Well I guess we will find out eventually." I think it was about a week later, we found out. We had a busy week and were headed to the barbeque after work on Friday. It was payday and we were ready to have a nice evening.

We were both excited about having the next day off. Sure enough, as we entered the barbeque area there were Hoyt and Cal. We told them that we were so relieved to see them. Cal said, "Well, not near as glad as we are to see you folks."

He said he and Hoyt would be by at 8:00 tomorrow morning to take us for a ride if it was okay with us. He said they had a lot to share and were meeting the other man on the team. I looked at him and said we would be ready. Hoyt was busy talking to Louise. Cal said, "It's a date. Let's party now."

The evening went great. Hoyt and Louise danced the first tune that Kenny, the fiddle player, and Rudy, the banjo man, were playing on stage. I could see that Louise liked Hoyt. I knew that he was a very exciting person and that I could not walk in his footsteps. He was living an exciting life style and I was definitely boring compared to Hoyt and his brother.

As I looked at them dancing I had kind of wished that we had not come out here. At that moment I was sorry that I had met the brothers. A little jealousy came over me for a few moments. But, after they finished that dance, I stood up at the table and Louise came right over to me and gave me a big hug and kiss. She said that the next dance would be mine. I was relieved and the jealousy subsided. I knew that she loved me, and I loved her so much that there was no way I could bear living without her at my side. I guess I had been a little silly to be jealous, but I decided that I would be sure to share my feelings again when we got to our rooms later that evening.

We had a great evening. Louise and I danced almost every dance. The only break we had from dancing was when the duet took a break. Both Hoyt and Cal met women and danced right next to us the whole evening. Right before the last tune Hoyt looked over at me and asked if I would give him dancing lessons. Louise said "If anyone can teach him to dance, it's you, Alec." We finished our drink and told him that we would see them in the morning. We told them that we were just simply too tired to go on, and headed for our room.

When we got there, I went out on the patio and Louise brought us both a glass of wine. As we drank the last of the wine and looked over the property Louise looked at me and told me that she truly loved me. I looked over at her and I told her that I could not live a minute more on this earth without her and that I also loved her more than anything else in this world. We kissed, finished our wine and went to bed. We made love and it was wonderful. It had to be the greatest moment of passion that I had ever experienced.

This woman was truly special. After making love we both crashed and the next thing we heard was the alarm waking us the next morning. We rose from our bed and smiled at each other and then finished dressing. We headed down stairs for breakfast. After breakfast we went over to the resort to meet our friends.

Chapter Eight
The Ride to the Mine

We had just arrived across the yard, in front of the resort when we saw them riding up. We walked over toward the gate at the west side to meet them. We arrived about the same time. We got up on the horses and Hoyt said that we were going to the mine. We rode down Castle Creek a little past the trail we had traveled the last time we went with them. Hoyt said we were going to the mine a different way. We started north and west and followed the wash for about four miles.

We came right up next to the mine and there waiting for us was a man sitting on a large rock by his horse holding the reins. He was about a hundred yards ahead of us. As we got closer he looked very familiar. Yes, it was Lance Alder, the deputy sheriff from Prescott. I thought we were in trouble for sure. As we approached he drew his gun and yelled halt to Hoyt. He said, "Come in slowly and keep your hands off your gun holsters."

I was definitely scared for myself, Louise, Hoyt and Cal. As we got within about thirty yards of him he told us to relax. He put his gun away. I was really surprised at the fact that Hoyt and Cal would be taken this easily but maybe they were considering the fact that Louise and I were with them. In any event we all got off of our horses. Lance shook Hoyt and Cal's hand. He asked Hoyt if we were the folks that they had spoken about. That is when it hit both Louise and I that this was the third person.

Hoyt looked over at us and said, "I bet you are surprised", and the three of them just laughed. We were surprised, but it explained a lot about how they were able to know about the jobs, and when it was safe to pull the jobs, having a man on the inside, so to speak. We all went into the mine and tied up our horses and headed back to the office, as Hoyt called it.

Hoyt went over to one of the Wells Fargo strong boxes and opened it, and there was their haul from the last job. Hoyt handed Lance $1,500 and said, "Here, feed your family and eat well until next time. We will wait for your orders as usual and we will meet you at the job."

Hoyt again looked at Louise and me. He then smiled at us, and pulled out a bottle of Tequila. He poured us all a shot. Lance looked at us and as we all raised our glasses he toasted the two new members of the gang. We were in whether we liked it or not now that we had met the mystery member of the gang. I looked over at Louise and she said, "Well I'm in." I smiled and said, "So am I."

Hoyt poured us another drink and then said that he wanted to explain the excitement they had after the past job that they pulled. He raised the glasses and made a toast to the fact that if Lance had not been with them that they would never have gotten here alive. Hoyt went on to explain that they had met Lance while they were stationed at the army stockade in Columbus, New Mexico.

Lance was an expert tracker and a long distance shooting marksman. He packed a Sharps 50 caliber rifle along with his pistol and a 30/40 Craig lever action rifle. Lance and Hoyt had become very good friends. After Lance got out of the service he became a lawman in Prescott. Lance looked at us and said, "You folks probably wonder what would cause a lawman to go astray." Lance told us that he had been a deputy for eight years. He had been through two different sheriffs and the last one was a joke.

The last sheriff had no experience as a lawman, and the election was strictly political. Lance had just been trying to support his family in Prescott, but the folks in Prescott would not vote to give him a raise. One night he ran into Hoyt and Cal, and they had spent an evening together at the Palace Bar, playing Faro, the predecessor of Black Jack.

Hoyt and Cal told Lance about their plans and said they could use a man like him to organize the robberies. They discussed their setup, and Lance decided to join them. Hoyt went on to explain that Lance was the one who helped them find the mine.

Hoyt went back to telling us about the rangers who were following them last week. "We got as far as South Mountain and rode to the top. We looked back and Lance spotted the posse about ten miles back. Lance said that it would be almost impossible to track us over the mountains."

"Lance said that he would give us a little time. He said that he would stay and frighten them off and that he would meet us later in Phoenix. We would meet at Tom's Tavern, which was around the corner from the San Carlos Hotel at midnight. He told us that he was best for the job and that there was no way for the posse to follow him by himself, but three horses would leave a trail. We said goodbye and took off."

"Lance stayed and shot at long distance to scare the posse and slow them down. Then, he headed down the mountain and then started back up towards the other side. He rode up to the posse and told them that he heard shots from the top of the mountain and went up to investigate. He told them that he had come from Phoenix and did not run into anyone on the way. He said that all he could figure was that if no one was going toward Phoenix that they must have come down and headed to Buckeye."

Hoyt took a drink of his whiskey and continued with his story. "The posse took off toward Buckeye and Lance showed up at the bar so whatever he said must have worked and boy, were we ever relieved. We spent the night at the hotel and headed for home the next morning. We had ridden so much that we decided to take the train. We loaded the horses on the cattle car and sat in the diner car for breakfast."

"Ironically, we sat next to a couple of Rangers, and I overheard one of them say that he had hoped that the train would be robbed while they were on it for this trip. I can guarantee you that we had indigestion after breakfast. We headed to the lounge and relaxed for the ride. We got off at Morristown and rode on into the ranch. As we rode that twenty-two miles we never spoke a word to each other."

"When we arrived at the ranch Lance told us that the last job cut it a little too close for comfort. He said that we needed to plan jobs a little closer to home in the future to reduce our chances of being caught. He said the Arizona Rangers were a very qualified group of lawmen."

Louise and I told Lance that we had read that one of the Rangers was on board the train that they robbed just north of Casa Grande. He met up with several more rangers when the train stopped in Casa Grande and they all took off after you guys. We just wondered how you all got away. Lance said, "It was a close call for sure, but they made it back."

Lance told us that he actually was at Hoyt and Cal's ranch the night before they interviewed us at the resort. He said he met the sheriff in the lobby. He told us that he sent a telegram to the sheriff asking to meet him at the resort to question the victims of the robbery. He told us he spent the night at Hoyt's ranch. Lance's main focus was to find out what we knew. He also wanted to know if the sheriff had any new leads. He was a very interesting guy.

Lance said they still needed to have us help them fence the goods. He felt that the Arizona Rangers would be close and they needed to change their system. We told him that we were both excited to be in the gang. He said that he also had a home down in Los Cabos. He went on to say that he was only three years away from getting a retirement settlement from the city. He was planning on moving his family down to Cabo right after he retired from active duty. We told him that hopefully we would already be there.

Lance said that when Colonel Vargas retired they would need someone down there that they could trust. He told us that they made a great haul, but that he was very concerned for all of them because they had gone outside the boundaries that they set for their jobs. He said that after this last job, they would stay in their territory. It was definitely safer in their area, that is, if any place is safe when you are outside the law.

He asked us if we were excited to get our personal belongings back, and he hoped that we did not say anything to anybody. We told him not to worry because we had indeed kept our mouths shut. He said that he enjoyed the talk that we had with the sheriff and he said it was obvious that we knew more. He also knew that we had our belongings back, and he hoped that we would keep quiet and we did. He said that he liked us right then. The fact that Hoyt and Cal trusted us meant a lot to him.

He was happy that we were in and he said that there was plenty to go around. He said that we would earn our share before it was all over. He thanked us and said that he was headed back to Prescott and his family. We all said goodbye to our new friend. Louise, myself, Hoyt and Cal headed back to the resort.

We were completely amazed at the intelligence of this gang. Hoyt told us on the way back to the resort that none of the posse had been hurt. He said that Lance was an incredible shot. He could hit what he wanted and miss what he wanted at a thousand yards. We were amazed when he pointed out how far one thousand yards actually is. He said it was easier when you are shooting from higher up. It is also a lot easier than shooting straight ahead on the ground for a thousand yards. We arrived at the resort and had lunch together and then we said goodbye to Hoyt and Cal. They said that they would see us for dinner.

We left and walked across the property to our room. We spoke along the way, and Louise expressed surprise about meeting the third person. She said that she was really surprised that he was one of the gang. It did not make sense but I guess a person must do what he must to feed his family. She went on to say that life was a lot harder out here and we were very lucky to have the job at the resort. She did say that we would simply eek out a menial life style and that if we wanted to get ahead their offer seemed to be great.

It appeared that we would not be subject to as much risk as the two brothers and Lance. I said that they were qualified to do their job, and we would be more qualified to move the stolen property. We would not draw attention to ourselves because we simply did not look suspicious. I told her that there are risks with anything when you gamble and this seemed to be the way to go. Louise said that she was behind me all of the way. I told her I would not even consider the new venture unless she totally agreed with it. I was excited when she stepped up to the pump in the mine.

We both had mixed emotions with regard to the whole situation. We really liked the three of them. We knew that they were wrong, but somehow we could sort of understand. This was a tough country and required tough men to survive. We looked forward to having dinner with them. We had hoped that Lance could be there so we could get to know him better but we understood that he had been away from his family and he was looking forward to seeing them.

Lance seemed like a good man, with a lot of family values. After listening to Hoyt and Cal, we were glad that he was in. We were both very surprised at our first meeting, though. Louise said that her heart was in her throat. I told her that I felt exactly the same. I thought we were going to be arrested. The excitement was beyond words. Our whole bodies stirred. It was probably due to the fact that we were considered part of the gang at that moment. Neither of us had ever experienced such movement that stirred us to our souls.

We could see why they enjoyed this work. There was just something exciting about doing something that we should not be doing. We looked forward to our trip to Mexico. In fact we were ready to go in with them, without even going down to Cabo. We just knew that they were for real. We rested the balance of the afternoon and then met them at the barbeque for dinner. We enjoyed another evening with our friends drinking, dancing and socializing. We had a very busy day and were very tired. Louise wanted to retire early. We left our friends at about 10 p.m. and called it an evening.

We said goodbye and Hoyt said that they would get in touch with us when the time came and just asked us to be ready. He said they had a lot of work ahead of them and they simply could not give us a definite time frame. We both looked at him, and at the same time we both said, "We'll be ready."

Chapter Nine
Alec Builds a Stable

We spent the next day Sunday relaxing around the resort and thinking about the gang. The manager, Jim Stanhouse, came up to us and said Hoyt and Cal suggested that we build a stable across the Castle Hot Springs road, which was to the west of the property. Jim said he wanted me to build the stable and when I finished he said that they were going to buy the horses and saddles from the brothers. Hoyt and Cal convinced him that I was the man for the job.

They told him that I was a little rusty but they knew that I knew horses. I told him that I had been in the cavalry in France during World War One. He showed me a set of plans and asked me if I could build the corral and stable. Jim said that he had already ordered the material and it would be delivered on the following Wednesday.

I had a lot to do, but I told him that I thought I could do the job. He said building the stable and corral was the more important job and he wanted it completed as soon as possible. He was surprised that someone had not come up with the idea of building a stable sooner. He thought it was a great idea. I was excited about the opportunity. I would be in charge of the stable and taking the visitors out on horseback rides.

The lumber arrived on schedule that next Wednesday. I was finished with the job by Saturday. The corral and the stable were ready for the horses. Jim said Hoyt and Cal would be over on Monday with the horses, saddles and a load of hay. Louise and I saw them at dinner on Saturday night and we all walked over to the stable and corral. Hoyt and Cal were impressed with my work. Hoyt looked at me and said, "Sir, you are a master of many trades and your diversity never ceases to amaze me or Cal." Hoyt said it would not take long to get everything set up on Monday.

They told us that they would be around at dawn so they could enjoy the great breakfast that was always served at the resort on Sunday. We spent the rest of the evening with Hoyt and Cal. We ducked out early because we both had a busy and tiring week. As we walked out, I turned to Hoyt and said, "We are ready whenever you are." He and Cal lifted their drinks and Hoyt said, "This one is for you. See you in the morning, my friend." We left for our rooms and hit the sack.

We were excited about the horses and equipment and the load of hay that was to arrive in the morning. It just seemed logical to have a stable for horseback riding for the guests. We both slept like babies and woke the next morning to the sounds of horses coming across the front of the property. We went out on the patio and watched the herd moving into the corral. They had two wagons following them. One was loaded with hay and the other carried saddles, bridles, reins and ropes. We got dressed as quickly as we could. We needed to get out to the corral to help them unload the wagons.

When we arrived they were already halfway through. Hoyt took us to the corral and introduced us to each of the ten horses that they brought. He told us about each of their personalities. Amazing, but they were all totally different. He said that I would become their trusted master.

I had been around horses but I never realized that they had a personality. I could see that he knew the horses and was right on the money about each of them. He told me how each one of them could be dealt with. He pointed to the roan and told me that I should ride that horse because the roan was the leader of the herd. We walked right up to the roan. I saddled the horse. I got up in the saddle and rode him. He was very responsive to the reins and even tempered, just as Hoyt had said.

He said that the pinto mare was perfect for Louise. It was the horse that they brought over both times that we went with the brothers. She said that she enjoyed riding the mare. Hoyt looked at me and said, "Well, this ought to keep you busy while we get everything together for the trip. Besides if you are going to live out here in the West you both had better get used to horses."

They finished unloading the hay and stacked the saddles in a locked tack room that was in the stable. We headed over to the restaurant and had breakfast. After breakfast Hoyt and Cal said goodbye and said they would see us in a couple of weeks. Lance had a job lined up for them. They spoke to us as we were walking them to the gate, so that nobody would overhear the conversation. We looked at them and thanked them for everything and wished them luck. We told them that our prayers would be with them.

They got on their horses and said adios. We waved goodbye and they rode off, headed toward their ranch. As it turned out, that would be the last time that we would see them for quite a while. They said that they had a lot of work to do and they felt like they had little time left. Hoyt said he felt that the law was getting close and this may be their last hurrah. Louise and I strolled across the lawn to our room.

I was very excited about being the new wrangler. What a joke, me from New York. Louise said we would have to go to town and get me a new wardrobe. At least I would look the part.

Chapter Ten
Hoyt and Cal Return

We both woke up early Monday morning. We ate breakfast and headed to work across the resort to our jobs. I kissed Louise and she went to her job as concierge. I walked across to the stable to feed the horses. I worked around the corral most of the morning, and I finished building the stable. Jim hoped that it would keep the horses out of the elements.

I broke away for lunch and met Louise at the deli inside the resort. We enjoyed each other's company over a sandwich. She asked me how the morning went and I told her that I was excited about this new responsibility. The manager had me scheduled to work at the corral in the mornings and I completed the rest of my jobs after lunch.

The week went by very quickly. We were both very busy with endless duties. I think it was on Friday that I was able to meet Louise again for lunch. When I arrived at the deli, Louise was already seated and was reading the paper.

She read that there was another robbery just outside of Prescott near a small town called Humboldt. There was not a lot of information on the robbery but the paper said it appeared to be the Ghost Riders. The paper indicated that the law enforcement agencies were getting very frustrated. There had been a reward posted for any information, that would lead to the arrest of these perpetrators. We both looked at each and smiled. Louise, being cautious, glanced around the room to be sure that the coast was clear before we proceeded to discuss the boys.

The coast was clear so she looked at me and said, "Well Alec, it looks like the boys are not wasting any time getting on with the program." The weeks seemed to fly by. There was no news of the gang, but I overheard the manager saying that he had heard there were several other robberies, but the press was told it was off limits to print any details. The law enforcement agencies did not want any more information to leak out about the gang and their methods.

Another week went by and we were both at the barbeque on Friday night for a steak fry. As we sat there drinking a beer and eating our steaks, we heard those familiar voices, and when we looked up both Hoyt and Cal were headed to our table. I could see Louise's eyes light up. I was also very excited to see them. We both worried about them while they were gone. It had been over a month since we saw them last.

They ordered their steaks and got a beer from the bar. They came over and asked if they could join us. We told them by all means. They sat down and Hoyt looked over at me and said, "Well Alec, how is the wrangling business?" I told him that I had been out on several rides with the guests. He teased, "And you didn't get lost?" I said, "Heck no, I just went on the same ride that you guys took us on up to the mine and around Castle Creek." I told him that I kept it simple.

He laughed and said that I was smart to keep the upper hand. That is the first rule of being a rancher - KISS. I said, "What is KISS?" He said, "Keep it simple stupid." We all laughed and continued drinking and dancing the rest of the evening.

Hoyt did tell us that they were ready to make the trip to Nogales to meet Colonel Vargas. I told him that I was pretty sure that we could go. He said that he wanted to go for a ride in the morning, and asked if we could be ready at 8 a.m. I told him that I had a group to take out for a ride in the morning. I asked him if we could do it on Sunday. He said that would be fine. We told him that we would be ready first thing Sunday morning.

We finished our last drink about eleven and we told Hoyt and Cal that we were just too tired to close the bar with them. I told him about all of the chores that were now part of our new job description. Hoyt said he understood and that they would see us tomorrow night for another steak fry. We said that we would meet them for sure.

Our morning ride went fine and we were back for lunch. Louise and I spent the rest of the afternoon resting in our room simply enjoying each other's company. It seemed that we were always so tired during the week. We really looked forward to the weekends and our lovemaking.

I would have thought that after all of that exercise that we would both would be exhausted, on the contrary. We were both starved and ready for a nice dinner and another evening of fellowship with friends. It sure makes for a nice evening when you have already had a meaningful afternoon.

It was about 5:30 when we started over to the barbeque. We ordered our steaks and I had a beer, Louise ordered a glass of wine. I looked over at her and whispered in her ear that I loved her and that she was truly a beautiful woman. I told her that I was the luckiest man in the world. She smiled and said that she felt the same way about me. She said that she was excited about the ride in the morning. I was too.

Just about then the boys walked in and went up to the bar. They ordered a drink and their steaks and then came over and joined us. Hoyt looked at Louise and said, "My, you look radiant tonight." She said that it was due to the fact that she had a great man for a husband and just smiled at me. He looked over at me and just smiled.

We enjoyed the rest of the evening again dancing and talking. We were both pretty intoxicated by midnight because those two cowboys would not let us buy a drink the whole evening. They continued to buy drinks until we were both tanked. We got up and midnight and said we would see them in the morning. We said goodbye and staggered across the property to our room.

We both were too drunk to do anything and when our heads hit the pillow we were gone. The alarm went off at seven in the morning. We each took a shower, dressed and went across the resort to they corral. I saddled up two horses for us and at about a quarter to eight Hoyt and Cal arrived. Hoyt looked at me and said, "Let's go. You lead. Take us to the mine." Off we went.

When we arrived, we went into the mineshaft and sat down. Hoyt showed us the take from all of the jobs. He asked us if we had gotten permission to leave for a couple of weeks. I told him that I had cleared the time off with Jim the resort manager. I told Jim that we had a family emergency and that we needed a couple of weeks off. I told him we would be leaving the next day, which was Monday, at 8 a.m. I told him that we were packed and ready to go.

He said there was a bus arriving in the morning, bringing a load of guests. He cleared it with the driver to take us back on the return trip to Morristown so we would be on time to catch the train. We all shook hands, and Hoyt poured us a shot of tequila. I asked him how Lance was doing. He said all was well with Lance. Lance said he was glad we were with them. We got back on our horses and rode back to the resort.

We arrived just in time for lunch again. We sat down and enjoyed a sandwich and then we said our goodbyes. We told them that we needed to pack for the trip and headed back to our room. We finished packing and then enjoyed each other's company the rest of the afternoon. We went to bed early in anticipation of the long day ahead.

Chapter Eleven
Our Trip and Future

We woke early the next day. We were both very excited about our trip. Jim, the resort manager, had agreed to give us a two-week leave of absence. We took our bags and hurried downstairs to eat breakfast before we left. We enjoyed our last meal with the crew before heading out to meet the shuttle bus.

We walked over to the front gate, and at about a quarter to eight Hoyt and Cal rode up on a buckboard driven by a friend. They got down and smiled as they greeted us. About 8 a.m. the bus drove up and proceeded through the gate to the front of the resort. The driver let the guests out and unloaded their baggage. He then drove the bus back out and picked us up at the gate.

We headed down the road to Morristown. The morning was beautiful as most mornings are beautiful in Arizona. We arrived at Morristown in no time, it seemed. Right about ten the train pulled up and we boarded. We ate our lunch as it pulled away heading for Phoenix, the first stop on the way to Nogales. We visited with Hoyt and Cal during the ride. We stopped again at Tucson to pick up additional riders. We left Tucson and arrived in Nogales just in time for dinner.

We got off the train and there was a Hispanic man wearing army clothes. Louise and I thought he might be Colonel Vargas, because of his apparel and the way that he carried himself. He just looked like a Colonel. It looked like he had an escort of soldiers with him. Hoyt got off the train first. He went right up and shook the officer's hand. We assumed then this was the Colonel Vargas that they had spoken so much about. He was not a very big man. I am just guessing but he was about five foot nine but he weighed somewhere around two hundred pounds. He had a moustache and was definitely well groomed. Hoyt called us over and introduced us to the gentleman. He bowed extended his hand in friendship and then invited us across the street for dinner. He said that he wanted to introduce us to a traditional Mexican dinner. We tried several Mexican beers to go with our great dinner.

Colonel Vargas told us that we needed to be at the train station by eight that night. He said the train would be leaving for Mazatlan almost immediately upon its arrival. He said that we would be riding all night and that we would reach our destination at dawn the next morning. The train arrived a few minutes late. We all boarded the train and we all fell asleep after the long day of traveling. There is something about a train ride that is actually very soothing. We both slept like babies even though we certainly were not very comfortable.

The train was not exactly a glorious ride. There were people with dogs, cats, birds and an assortment of other animals. Hoyt looked over at me and said "Alec, unique huh? These people live a little different down here. There is no middle class in Mexico. The people are either very rich or very poor. We were a little surprised just like you folks when we came down here our first time."

We arrived at Mazatlan early the next morning right at dawn. The place was everything that Hoyt and Cal they said. It was just as they described the evening that we enjoyed drinks and conversation at the resort. It was semi-tropical with a lot of greenery. It was totally different than the terrain we left in Arizona. We boarded a ship at the dock. We arrived at the island in about one hour. The island was just as beautiful as Hoyt and Cal had explained earlier. We were both completely in shock. It truly was paradise. The home looked to be everything that they promised it would be. We could see the home at the top of a hill in the distance.

We arrived after a short ride. The Colonel showed us around the home and we all sat down on the patio that overlooked the bay. It was truly gorgeous.

Colonel Vargas introduced us to all of the people in the network. We spent a couple more days on the island relaxing and enjoying the view and the weather. Every morning it would rain a little but it never lasted and the sun was usually out by eleven o'clock. We all really enjoyed the fishing trip. They took us out for a full day and we caught so many fish that we were dead tired when we arrived back for dinner. The Colonel told us that fishing was the main stay of the folks on the Island.

Later that evening the Colonel took us to a little town about a mile and a half from the villa. This town was definitely a fishing village. There were a lot of fresh fish markets in the town. There were also a lot of quaint little shops in the market place. The Colonel said that when the tuna are running again the town would explode. He said we were there during the slow season.

When we arrived back from the fishing trip the Colonel took us past the front of the Villa and about three hundred yards east of the main villa that belonged to Hoyt and Cal. There was another beautiful villa that was hidden by all of the vegetation. It actually was on property adjacent to the property owned by the guys. It was a little smaller but every bit as beautiful and comfortable as their Villa. It was far enough away that it was quiet and was not visible from their Villa. It also had a beautiful view of the beach from the back porch. The Colonel told us that this villa would be ours permanently, if we decided to work with them. It was far enough away that we would have our own privacy.

Later that evening, which was our last night, before we were to begin our trip back to the US, the Colonel took us into the village to a local restaurant and we had a wonderful dinner. The Mexican people love to dance. They were up dancing all night, from little children to grandparents. The Colonel walked out on the pier and came back with a large bag of fish. He said that the fishermen were very generous and shared their catch with friends.

The Colonel told us that we would need to go back to Castle Hot Springs and ready ourselves because he wanted us to transition the next month, if we were ready. He said that his time to retire had arrived and he was ready. He said interestingly enough, he was only about a mile away on the same island. He told me that he knew there was no place on earth he would rather spend the rest of his life than right there. I looked at Louise and said that is good enough endorsement for us. We told him we would be ready.

We boarded the train and headed back to the US to get our lives in order. We would need to contact our folks and let them know about our next big move. This move would seem a lot easier because we had already put such a distance between us. Because we had made such a big move from New York to Arizona, this move was really minor league. We did not want to leave the Island. It was so quiet, peaceful and beautiful, all we could think about was being right there on the island. We arrived back in two days. The time went by fast, it seemed, on the train ride back to the border. We were full of anticipation about the move.

The manager at the resort was happy that we came back earlier than expected. He said that he did not realize how much they needed us, and did not realize how much work we actually performed for them. We told him that we had made a huge decision. We were giving him a month's notice that we would be leaving. We thought that a month would give him time to replace us. He was very thankful and he was also happy for us. He said that everybody would miss us but that he understood that we needed to move on with our lives.

We headed to our room to prepare for our last month. It was hard to believe that in less than a year that we had come all the way out here to Arizona. Now we were ready to make another big move. As we walked across the property, I looked at Louise and said, "I was a little apprehensive about coming to Arizona." I told her that I had come to like Arizona but I love it down there now. I told her that I was really excited about this next move. I did not know if I could contain myself for the next month. Louise said that she also could hardly wait to settle into our new life.

Louise looked over at me and said that she was also just as excited about the move as I. She told me that she also would have to work at staying focused for the next month. We hit the sack early that night so we would be ready for the next day of work. We both discussed the whole situation over and over. It seemed like hours before we finally fell asleep.

The next morning we woke early again, showered, and went into the kitchen and had breakfast. Afterward we headed across the property and as we approached the entrance the manager came out and met us. He said that there were guests to take on a ride that morning and that they would be ready at 9 a.m. He handed me a pistol in a holster. I asked him what the gun was all about. He said that the snakes were coming out of hibernation and that the gun was loaded with buck shells to kill the snakes.

He said that this was a dangerous time for horseback riding. I looked at Louise and said "amazing it is April already!" I told Jim, the manager, that I was not exactly a great shot. He said "That is why the shells are buckshot, so even you can't miss." I said okay and strapped on the holster. Louise laughed and so did I. I looked the part of a cowboy but nothing could be farther from the truth. I kissed Louise and headed for the corral to get the horses ready for the guests. As I readied the horses, my mind wandered to the quaint island and the people of the village. I was so excited about our upcoming life.

The weeks just seemed to fly by. We did not hear anymore about the "Ghost Riders' because the paper was not allowed to print any updates. I knew that the reward was still posted. We did not see Hoyt and Cal for about two weeks. It was a Friday night after a long hard week. We headed to the barbeque at the resort. We walked in and there were Hoyt and Cal sitting at our usual table.

Hoyt, who is the louder of the two stood up and waved us over. He said he already ordered us a drink. Louise went over and hugged them both and sat down at the table. I went over to the bar and ordered our steaks and then went over and joined the brothers at the table. We laughed and talked. Hoyt leaned over and asked me quietly if we were ready. He said they had been bringing in a lot of loot this past month. They hoped that they might only have to continue for another month. If it kept up for one more month at this pace, they would be set.

I told him quietly that we were ready for anything that they needed. He asked me if we could join them in the morning for another ride. I told him that I had a group of guests to take out for a morning ride but that we could be ready after lunch. He said fine. We partied the rest of he evening. I noticed that Louise enjoyed dancing with Hoyt. I was not jealous anymore because I knew how she felt about me. He was a handsome man and was a very exciting person for sure. I told Louise at 8:00 that I was too tired to continue, and that I had the early morning ride.

Hoyt looked over and said to Cal, "Can you believe it? Alec is a wrangler." He said, "Alec, you are quite a guy. Louise is a lucky girl." I smiled and thanked him and then told Louise that she could stay if she wanted to. She smiled and grabbed my hand and said, "Let's go". We said goodnight and headed for our room.

Upon arriving in our room, Louise took out a bottle of wine that she had been saving and opened it and poured us both a glass. We sat on the upper outside patio holding each other's hand. After the glass of wine, we retired to the bed and made love. The morning came early.

Louise leaned over and planted a big kiss on my lips, and told me that she loved me. I repeated the words back to her. We got dressed and went down for breakfast again. The great breakfasts that Angelica cooked would surely be missed by both of us.

We went across the front of the property. There were already folks enjoying the healing waters of the spas even this early in the morning. I kissed Louise goodbye and she headed into the resort as I headed out the road to the west of the property. I went through the gate across the road to the stable, which was about five hundred yards from the resort. I overheard the manager tell the security guard that they were expecting a bus from Morristown at around noon with some new guests and that he was to detain the driver because there were folks that were heading back to Morristown after their vacation.

I guess it was about 8:00 when the guests showed up. I helped them saddle their horses and then I lead them out toward the mine. I always liked taking folks to the Copperopolis mine because it was in such great shape and there was so much history attached to the mine. Half of the buildings were still there. It was like a ghost town. The guests seemed to enjoy the ride.

We arrived at the mine at about 9:00 and spent an hour walking around while I explained all about the mine and gold mining procedure. I sounded like an expert thanks to Hoyt and Cal. They definitely taught me well. As long as the guests were happy that was all that counted.

We left at about 10:00 and headed back to the resort a different way. We went down the other side of the mine and went back by way of the wash. As we approached the resort riding down Castle Creek wash, we heard what sounded like gunshots. Sure enough, just then, my horse bucked and right below the horse was a rattlesnake.

I drew my gun and shot the snake. He was dead for sure. I was very thankful that the bullets were snake load. Snake load is a 22 shell with buckshot instead of solid lead. It is strictly for killing snakes. I could never have hit that cuss with a regular pistol load. Needless to say the guests were thankful. I told them that the shooting was probably other folks killing snakes. This was the time of the year that they come out of hibernation and are very aggressive. I guess we would be aggressive if we had not eaten in five months.

As we came about a quarter of a mile from the resort, I noticed ahead that the resort bus was stopped in the road and there were several men around the bus with guns drawn. It appeared that the bus was in the process of being robbed. I stopped the guests from going any closer to protect them. I told them that I would go ahead quietly and when the coast was clear that I would come back for them. I kind of laughed to myself because I was sure I knew the robbers.

As I approached I looked a little closer, and I noticed something was not right. There were at least six men, not three, and they looked Hispanic. I stopped dead in my tracks when I realized that I did not know these men. It was too late. One of the men saw me and drew down on me asking me to come in with my hands held high. He told me to pull my gun and drop it. I told him that it was just a pea-shooter just for killing snakes.

As I pulled the pistol, one of the other banditos fired and hit me in the lower right of my chest just at the junction of my lower two ribs. The force of the shell knocked me off of the horse. I could not believe how much pain I felt. The leader hollered at the gang and told them to hold their fire. He told them that he had the situation in hand and that there was no need to shoot anybody. Great statement, but it was a little too late for me since I was already laid out on the ground with a bullet in my chest. It definitely was not much of a relief when the head of the gang came over and apologized for the incident before leaving the robbery scene. He said that if I could get back to the resort that I had a chance of making it.

I took no consolation in his words and wished that the gun I had was a 44, but this little 22 would not do any good. The pain was excruciating and my life was passing before my eyes. I could not believe that we had come all of this way and we were right on the brink of paradise and now this had to happen. The banditos took off and the bus driver and some of the folks came over and helped me onto the bus. The guests rode up and followed us to the resort.

By the time we arrived at the resort, I had lost a lot of blood. The driver hollered for help as we arrived and the manager and the rest of the staff came running. He said that they had been robbed and that I tried to save the folks. I was thankful but at this point I just wanted to live. Louise came running, crying and yelling, "What happened to Alec!" When she arrived she grabbed me and hugged me. I told her that I was not afraid and then I told her that I thought it was too late for me.

She cried and hugged me tighter. I told her not to cry, that everything would be alright. I told her that my life with her had been great. There was a doctor, who was a guest, and he came right over and started working on me. They carried me to a room in the back of the resort and the doctor continued to work on me. I just was in so much pain that I asked the doctor if he could help the pain. He gave me something but it did not matter.

Louise continued to hold me. I heard the doctor tell Louise that he had done all that he could. He said I had lost a lot of blood. There was no way that they could get me anywhere to obtain blood. Hoyt and Cal arrived and came up to Louise and hugged her. I heard Hoyt ask what happened. Louise said that she really did not care what happened. The only thing that mattered was that she was losing her husband. The next thing that I knew was that everything went black. I could still hear the people around me but I could not see.

I overheard Hoyt say to me that he and Cal would take care of Louise for the rest of her life. He made the promise to me saying that this was the least they could do for such a great guy and such a good friend. He told me that he was very sorry about everything. I heard them all talking about me as the doctor continued to work on me. I was still able to hear them for quite a while. I had no feeling though in my body. All I could think of was my beautiful Louise.

Chapter Twelve
The Trip Back to New York

The next morning Hoyt and Cal helped load Alec's body on the Morristown Bus, which would carry him to Phoenix and then on to New York, which would be his final resting place. Louise woke the next morning, Wednesday, April 25, 1921. She headed down to the kitchen for a cup of coffee and a roll. Ironically the San Carlos Hotel was the first place they stayed when they arrived in Arizona.

She finished the coffee and roll and boarded the trolley. The trolley stopped at several locations including the San Carlos hotel where she was staying, but arrived at the train station with plenty of time to spare. When she got off the trolley there waiting at the train station was the coroner and Dr. Randolph. They pointed to one of the cars and told her that Alec was aboard and ready for the trip.

They both kissed her right hand and led her to her car. Dr. Randolph told her that he had already secured her seat and berth and he wished her well. Within a few minutes the train pushed east. The ride took five days and reached New York on April 30th. Louise wrote in her diary.

It was the longest ride of my life. I could not help but think of my loving husband on the train with me but not being able to spend time with him. There was a huge hole in my heart. When we arrived at NY Central train station, my parents and both of Alec's parents were waiting at the station. The hearse was also there to transport Alec to our neighborhood mortuary. We watched them load Alec's body and then we headed for home.

We all sat around upstairs above the butcher shop looking at old pictures of Alec and myself. We all hugged each other. I opened a small suitcase and took out recent pictures. The folks were excited to see the pictures. Alec's mother and father hugged me and told me they were so glad that I was home. I told them how proud they should be of Alec. I explained he had built a stable and corral, and learned how to be a horseman. They were a little shocked. Alec's dad said that he was happy that his son had been able to experience the greatness of the west and that it appeared that he grabbed for all of the gusto.

He said that my job was open at the dry cleaners when I was ready. I told him I was now trained to work in the hotel business as a concierge. He asked what a concierge was. I told him that I helped guests by showing them where all of the sites were and also pointing out special programs. Dad said it sounded like a fun job. I told dad that I would be pursuing this position after the funeral, which would be Friday May 1st. The funeral went as well as could be expected. Most of the neighbors and the friends we grew up with were all there.

I explained that the West was totally different. The feeling of neighbors and neighborhoods really did not exist for all practical purposes. During the funeral I could not help but wonder how Hoyt, Cal and Lance were doing. I hoped that all was going good for them. I really missed the west and them. I told the folks that there was beauty in the west even though our life had ended so abruptly.

We all took our consolation in the fact that our Alec died a hero trying to protect others. I started looking for work about a week later. I felt that I needed to work to help keep my mind and heart from breaking. I was able to secure a job at a large upscale hotel within a week. The money was good but it certainly was not Castle Hot Springs. I was reading the Arizona Republic one morning on my coffee break to see how it was going out in the west.

On the second page I saw an article about the capture of three men for the murder of a Castle Hot Springs employee, Alec Centro. The article went on to say that the deputy sheriff from Prescott and two other deputies cornered the men in a mine close to the Resort. I guess they had been hiding out in the mine.

One of the deputies tracked them to this mine. There was a gunfight and two of the robbers were killed. Two of the deputies were wounded but not seriously. The two remaining robbers would stand trial for murder. As I read I had mixed emotions. I was happy that these perpetrators were caught but was unhappy not knowing which of my friends was injured. I was happy that the killers were in custody, but it was not going to bring back my Alec. I had hoped that the wounds were not serious and hoped that Hoyt, Cal and Lance were okay.

There was a special place in my heart for Hoyt and the gang. I could not deny it. I remembered in my grief kissing Hoyt. I felt tremendous love coming from within him. I felt the same way about him. I had such mixed emotions. I just never wanted to admit the possibility. I just wondered if it was possible to love two men so much in one lifetime. Whether I ever see Hoyt again, it will not change the way he stirs my soul.

I found myself checking out books from the library about Mazatlan, Mexico and the surrounding area. I was never able to find anything about the island we visited. I showed pictures to the folks and when they would ask me about the islands location I could only draw from memory.

About three months later, sometime in July, I was at work, and I received a call from the front desk. The deskman indicated that there was a man out front to see me. My heart stirred for reasons that I could not explain. As I opened the door there at the desk was Hoyt. He smiled at me and I fainted right on the spot. When I came to, he was holding me and asked me if I was okay. I looked into his eyes and knew that I had missed him greatly. It was a different kind of feeling than what I had with Alec.

Hoyt hugged me and gave me a kiss. His kiss really stirred my whole being from my toes to my lips. When I kissed him he was totally taken back. He looked at me and said, "You mean that you feel the same way about me? " I looked up at him and said a big "Yes." He said he did not come for that reason, but it was all that he could do to continue the rest of his days without thinking about me. He said that he, Cal and Lance were all fine. He said that they had retired from their work and looked at me smiling and said "you know the work."

He went on to say that once Alec's killers were caught in our hideout that the game was over. The "Ghost Riders" simply retired without incident. One of the robbers had heard of the hideout from some of Pancho Villa's men and knew they would be safe there. He said that once the location was discovered that there was no way the Ghost Riders could continue.

Besides, he said that they now had a streak of honesty. He said that Lance retired from the sheriff's office. He sold his property in Los Cabos. Hoyt said that Lance bought a cattle ranch outside of Prescott near Peoples Valley. Hoyt said that when their parents passed away, he and Cal sold the ranch. He said they got enough money from the sale to enable them to move down to their property on the Island. Then he smiled and said that he had hoped that I remembered the place.

He extended his hand, held mine, and said that the island was not the same without me there with them. He asked me if I would consider going back to Mexico with him. He said that the home adjacent their property was still there and it belonged to her. Then he smiled and said that really he wanted me to come back as Mrs. Hoyt Clancy. He wanted to give me the option of living in the other home but he just needed to have me near him for the rest of his life. I knew that New York was my home and really beautiful, but I missed our island. I looked at him, and said, "Yes, I will be Louise Clancy."

We went back to my house and I introduced Hoyt to my parents, and told them that I was going back to the island with Hoyt, because I loved him. My father said, "We'd like to come out and visit." I looked at my father and said, "If you come out you will never leave." My parents invited Hoyt to stay with us until we finalized our plans. Hoyt told my parents that all he knew was that he was financially set and loved their daughter more than life itself. My father looked at him and said, "That is good enough for me and your mom."

My father then asked him if there was room for them on this island paradise. Hoyt looked right into his eyes and said, "You bet. Since Louise and I have decided to get married, the other villa is ready and waiting for you folks. There will always be room for the father and mother of Louise and my dear friend Alec's parents as well. Before I leave, I want to meet Alec's parents. Alec was one of the greatest men that I have ever known. His diversity amazed us all."

We met with Alec's parents the next day. Hoyt praised their son stating that he would take care of me for the rest of his life and he owed it to Alec to follow through with his promise. Everybody likes Hoyt. He simply has a very real effect on everybody he meets. He is handsome, about six foot two, and about two hundred pounds, with blue eyes and dishwater blond hair. It is his piercing eyes that are the telltale of his soul.

We were married the next day and got on the train heading for Tucson an hour after the wedding. The trip seemed short even though it took five days. We were both dead tired and worn out when we arrived. I would never have dreamed that a honeymoon on a train could be so beautiful and intense at the same time. He was a tremendous lover. He said that I brought out the animal in him. He said he had never felt that way about anyone in his life.

We boarded the train outside of Tucson and headed for Nogales and then on to Mazatlan. We were both happy that there were no berths of beds on the train through Mexico. We both needed the rest. He was a perfect gentlemen. It was me that wanted him every minute of every day. I could not believe that I felt this way about him. I had definitely loved Alec, but this whole experience was totally different.

Hoyt kept saying that he had something very important to show me on the island. I kept wondering what could be so important. I would have thought that our love was plenty. I know that it was all that I could think of. We arrived early the next morning riding again all night with the peasants and a couple of geese. We were so tired that we slept right through the whole trip. We boarded the boat and headed to the island. Hoyt seemed to be in a hurry to get to the island. He was a man on a mission and I was very happy. When we arrived at the island there was Cal waiting for us. He helped unload our luggage and gave me a big hug and kiss. He told me that he was very glad that I had decided to come back with his brother. Hoyt introduced me as Mrs. Hoyt Clancy. He was very excited for both of us.

As we approached the house, he stopped the carriage out in front of the entrance. Cal and Hoyt helped me down off the carriage. They both held me and they said that they had something special to show me. Hoyt said the walk would not take long. We followed a trail to the left of the home and went to the beach Alec liked to visit. We know that wherever Alec is right now, he is listening to the waves. I cried for the next two hours. He looked at me and said that he owed it to Alec to take care of me the rest of his life and he could not wait for the journey. My parents came to visit the next year. Then they moved out to the island permanently two years later. We both lived there the rest of our lives. Life was very relaxing and we were able to raise three children. We never discussed the "Ghost Riders" again.